An Innocent Affair

by

Susannah Pope

Grosvenor House
Publishing Limited

This book is published by
Grosvenor House Publishing Ltd
28-30 High Street, Guildford, Surrey, GU1 3HY.
www.grosvenorhousepublishing.co.uk

A CIP record for this book
is available from the British Library

ISBN 978-1-907211-80-5

For Peter, Percy and Mark;
for keeping me sane

CHAPTER ONE

As he was led away in handcuffs my whole world collapsed.

I knew from the moment I saw him that he was going to be extraordinary. I was a teacher straight out of training. I was 21. He was 17. I had accepted a post teaching English literature in a remote, rather old fashioned boarding school on the edge of the Yorkshire moors. The day I travelled there it rained continuously and the wind whistled loudly through the trees. The skies were dark, almost angry. By the time I reached Hawksmoore station, my destination, it was black, cold and rather eerie.

I was met by an American, a young athletic looking man who seemed barely out of his teens. He was standing next to a 1950's racing green open-top Morgan sports car. He smiled warmly and apologised in advance for the impending uncomfortable, wet ride to the school. His name was Chad. He looked like he could have taught physical education as he was quite muscular and indeed quite healthy looking. I was surprised to learn however that he taught maths. I took an instant liking to him. He seemed genuine and kind. He was very eager to talk and to listen. As he drove the wet was beginning to seep through our clothes. He chatted about his background, that he was actually educated in England.

I was curious to know about the other members of staff as I had only met the Headmaster at my interview. I was only one of two women who worked at the school. The other woman was the school matron, Margaret Simms. According to Chad she had been there nigh on twenty years. She had a reputation for being nosey and interfering. She was also grossly overweight, had a rather large bosom and spoke with a severe Scottish accent. I was particularly looking forward to meeting her. We must have driven for about half an hour when a saw the school in the distance.

"Why come here to teach?" he asked. "We're in the middle of nowhere. It is just up ahead."

"Sorry," I replied. I couldn't hear anything above the sound of the car and the sound of the wind and rain.

"Why take a job here?" he shouted at me.

"I'm just out of training. My mother and brother live in York and I need to be close to them. My brother Edward is autistic. He is a lot for my mother to cope with especially since my father died."

"Geez I'm so sorry. How old is your brother?"

"He's my twin. I love him dearly but he can be hard work even at the best of times." I don't know why I felt such a compunction to tell Chad all this, after all I had only know him a matter of minutes. We arrived at the incredibly stunning, imposing building wet through at around 8pm. I had been due to have arrived at 6pm for the staff meeting but not surprisingly my train had been delayed.

The school itself was a profoundly large country house. Ivy crawled over its walls and the small lattice windows gave the impression of a family home, probably built, I guessed, around 1900. It was a country house straight out of a Jane Austen book. The house in summer was according to Chad stunning but on this night I was just could not wait to be inside. We were met at the door by Miss Simms. Chad's description of her could not have been more accurate.

"This is Mary Kendall, Margaret" said Chad looking at me with a huge smile on his face. I looked a mess. My hair was sopping and terribly windswept from the lack of roof on the car.

"We were expecting you at 6pm," she said annoyed.

"Yes, I'm afraid the train was terribly delayed."

"Well you've missed dinner."

"No matter I'm not hungry," I replied.

"Mr Elson will show you where the kitchen is. You may find something there." Chad pointed his finger at himself to show to whom she was referring.

"Thank you, Margaret."

"Miss Simms, if you will." Chad gave a smile of delight.

"Oh, of course. Sorry, Miss Simms."

"I'll take your bags to your room, Mary. It's on the top floor. There are no boys on that floor so you should find it a little more private." I couldn't wait to get out of the wet clothes and curl up in a nice warm bed. "I'll show you up there."

"Thanks." I followed him up at least four flights of stairs.

"Sorry about Margaret. Most of us just ignore her. She has been here for many years and seen five new head-masters and God only knows how many teaching staff. She is part of the furniture now. Quite literally." He laughed, sensing my feelings of unease.

"What an awful woman," was all I could say in response. I should have been more charitable but I was too tired and too wet to care. I followed Chad up to the fourth landing. The lighting was minimal; it was like we had gone back to the Victorian era. We passed many walls of photographs, old pictures and wooden shields celebrating those boys who had achieved great results in the world of sport and academia.

"Through here, Mary." He led me down a small passage-way, the floor boards creaked and a slight draft was blowing through the small set of windows.

"We save on lighting here. You may have noticed it is rather primitive. We have our own generator which suits us pretty well. You'll get used to it. Hot water is available between 7pm and 9 pm and from 7.30 until 8.30 am. Your expression tells me you weren't told about this. We are relatively self sufficient. There are paraffin lights, if you want one, and of course candles and torches. The boys are not allowed candles. Too many curtains on fire from previous years."

"No. No, they didn't tell me," I sighed.

Most of the boys would arrive tomorrow apart from a select few who arrived early due to parents keen to deliver their offspring as soon as they could. We arrived at my rooms. There was a small sitting room, with a small upright piano, a small bedroom area, where, once through the door, you had to move yourself around so the door could close behind you. Finally there was a very small bathroom. It did however contain a small Victorian free standing bath which was deep and inviting.

"Right, I'll leave you to, well, do whatever ladies do. Staff meeting is at 9am in the Headmaster's office. I'll say goodnight then. Sleep well."

"Thank you, Chad."

"I'll see you in the morning," said Chad as he closed the door behind him

I sat down on the bed and looked around at my new home. I had enough time to run the bath before the witching hour. I let myself soak until my fingers became pruned and I finally made it into bed around 9.30. It was eerily quiet inside the house as well as outside. The rain had stopped but the wind was still whistling. Apart from the obvious nerves about my first teaching post, I had to admit this quietness and solitude were beginning unnerve me.

The next morning, I was awoken however by the sun streaming through my curtains. The moors looked so different in the sun. The disquiet I felt from last night gradually began to fade. The boys also would arrive that morning which I was looking forward to immensely. I'd only met Chad and Miss Simms and, of course, the Headmaster who had interviewed me. All of Bramleigh's teaching staff had been male up till now. I wondered how I would be seen, the school was definitely old fashioned but I hoped they would take to me as much as Chad.

I slipped into a seat at the back of the Headmaster's office for the staff meeting and was extremely pleased when Chad slid into the chair next to me. "Hi Mary, did you sleep well?"

"Hi Chad, I slept really well thanks. It is very quiet here."

"You get used to it. It may take a while but you do get used to it."

In walked the Headmaster, Mr Hanrahan. He was a tall, slim and an attractive man who in his prime must have been a real hit with the ladies. Here, however he looked austere and quite sombre.

"Good morning everyone. Firstly I'd like to mention two changes in staff this term: Miss Kendall, who will be teaching English, and Mr Freeman, who will be teaching Chemistry." Mr Freeman looked like he had been caught in one of his own experiments and seemed so old that I thought he might not make it to the end of the meeting. Chad gave me a friendly nudge and an understanding smile.

Mr Hanrahan read through the school notices, highlighting boys who may need academic or pastoral help. It wasn't until he got to the end of the "Naughty boys" list that I became intrigued.

"Michael Moorcroft's foster parents have refused to take him over the long weekends and shorter school holidays. He will remain in school until the end of term next year. Miss Simms will organise him at these times."

There were general groans and muttered moans from most of the staff.

I looked around and turned towards Chad. He leant closer to me.

"That kid has been pushed around for the last seven years. No one takes responsibility for him. He's been through four foster homes. He's a great kid, high spirited perhaps, but a great kid," he whispered.

"Sorry, Mr Elson, do you have something to say," barked the Headmaster.

"No Sir, just filling in Miss Kendall."

"Kindly do so in your own time."

"Yes, Sir," he smirked.

The Headmaster continued, "As I was saying, Moorcroft must be given an attendance slip in each class. He must remain in your class until the end of the lesson. Failure to show up must be reported immediately. Miss Kendall if this boy is disruptive in any way, you will not be expected to deal with him. You will send him to me straight away."

Who on earth was this boy and what had he done to warrant such anger and attention. I was intrigued. I expected there would be some rotten apples amongst the boys but this seemed to fit the description of an old fashioned juvenile delinquent. Not allowed this, not allowed to do that. I had a vision in my head of what I expected this boy to look like. A thug? A monster?

"Also before we finish the meeting, under no circumstances is Moorcroft allowed to leave the school grounds. Period," continued the Headmaster.

After the meeting we all went out to greet the boys and their parents as they arrived. A couple of younger boys were terribly upset and caught solace in the over large bosom of Miss Simms for a few seconds of comfort. I got the feeling as I stood at the front door that someone was watching me. I looked up and there was. At the window of one of the boys' dormitories was the figure of a boy staring down at me. I couldn't make out the face but he seemed to be one of the older boys. I felt his presence until all the boys had arrived. I took a quick glance upwards as I went to move into the house and there he still stood seemingly watching my every move. Feeling uncomfortable I briefly stopped in the staffroom. Luckily Chad was there and seemed to sense my unease.

"Hi, Mary. You sure look like you have seen a ghost."

"Chad, there was a boy just standing staring out at me from the dormitory," I said slightly alarmed.

"Great! Now you have seen our famous boy. He does it every time term ends and begins. He is always left here. We just ignore it now. Sorry you should have been warned. It is a little disconcerting."

"Yes. Just a little," I lied.

The school now became alive with the chatter and noise of the boys. Every now and then there would a colossal "Do not run" from various teachers moving to and from their classrooms. I would meet the rest of the boys at supper. The school only had sixty pupils and by the second week I knew practically all their names. Supper was at 6.30 followed by prep at 7.00. As I was the only female teacher on the staff I wondered what the boys' reaction would be to me. I nervously left my rooms at 6.20 and made my way to the dining hall. Thankfully I saw my saviour, Chad, wave at me. The dining hall was just as imposing and ornate as the rest of the house. Above the top table was a large coat of arms displaying the school code: "Diligence and Discipline." I took my seat and felt sixty sets of eyes staring at me. It was the older boys that slightly unnerved me. I was only 21. These boys were only four or five years younger than I. The Headmaster walked in. The boys stood up, scraping their chairs on the wooden floor. Silence prevailed. He sat down, followed by the boys, and began to read the school notices.

"We have two new members of staff this term, Mr Freeman, on my right and Miss Kendall on my left. Please make them welcome to our family."

I was thankful that we were not made to stand or my embarrassment would have been visibly evident. As we began to eat my eyes focused on a senior boy sitting nearest to me on the pupils' table. I felt like I had seen him before. It was him I saw. He was the face at the window. The Moorcroft boy. I was quite unprepared for his appearance as I looked closer at him. His face was incredibly beautiful, somewhat like a girl's. He had a totally symmetric face with a jaw line so pronounced that it looked like it could cut granite. He ran his fingers through his thick tousled hair, looked up and smiled a wide smile at me.

I tried to avoid eye contact with him throughout supper. Luckily Chad was on hand to keep my mind, and eyes, at bay. Michael would be in my first class tomorrow morning. First impressions do count but I thought that impression there would be the real test.

At 8.45 I walked into my classroom. Nothing compares to the safety of teacher training than your first encounter as a qualified teacher. I took some deep breathes and pulled myself together. And then I saw him sitting alone. I was caught off guard and could only display what could be described as a grimace at him.

"Good morning Miss, I'm Michael Moorcroft," he beamed. He stood up, ran his fingers through his hair and extended his hand to shake mine.

As the saying goes my heart seemed to skip a beat. I felt the blood rush to my cheeks and I became embarrassed by my presence, his presence and the palpable silence that existed between us. He broke that silence.

"I'm sorry if I scared you. I like to be punctual for class." I limply shook his hand and muttered a very quiet good morning back to him.

"Where are your classmates?" I pulled myself together, "I like my students to be punctual."

"Oh they'll be here."

I sat down at my desk willing myself not to look at the boy before me. Minutes later the other boys arrived. It was small class of six. They were all keen, all curious and all hormonal. I deliberately toned down my wardrobe wearing something unrevealing and conserva-tive. I was thinking along the lines of a convent girl. I chose Hamlet, William Shakespeare, for the chosen text, ignoring the popular Romeo and Juliet, thereby avoiding embarrassment with the questions of love and eventual sex. One thing I knew for certain was that Michael Moorcroft was going to prove very interesting to teach. Something about that boy made you lose your-self for a moment.

The staffroom at lunch was a sombre affair: several bald-ing old men, forever bachelors, hunched over the Times' crossword and smoking from antique pipes. I had noth-ing in common with these people. They barely looked up when I walked in and had no time for pleasantries. Chad was not far behind me and it was nice to be able to talk about my morning.

"How did it go, Mary?"

"They are very keen to learn; which is such a blessing."

"Yes, but what about him?" he urged.

"Him?" I knew exactly to whom he was referring.

"Moorcroft! Of course."

"Oh fine. He was very welcoming. He seemed like a decent, friendly young man."

"You know I like the kid but don't be fooled Mary by his charm. He can manipulate very well. Proceed with caution. That is all I'm saying. He has a small posse who follow his every move."

"He's just a boy."

"Please tread carefully around him. Okay?"

I beamed a false smile at him and said I would. I had two free periods that afternoon so went to explore the staff garden. The torrential rain over the last few days had made the smell of the last of the flowers ever sweeter. I really missed by boyfriend Robert. He was a concert pianist on a European tour. His way of living seemed to fit in with my lifestyle here. We met after a concert he was giving as we both hailed a taxi in the pouring rain. He was kind and gentle, a real gentleman. We got engaged last spring.

The weeks went by and I was far more confident in myself and in my teaching. Chad had become my confidante and indeed my friend. Miss Simms seemed the bully she was deemed to be and was terribly interfering with staff and pupils alike. Being surrounded by crusty old men for years had obviously taken its toll. She had become an honorary male. She expressed no femininity and had no wish for me to show mine.

CHAPTER TWO

The autumn term was well underway and the rugby season began. Every boy was supposed to participate. Although our school was situated on the edge of the moors, an ample, but very rough rugby field was laid out. I made no bones about pretending to know the first thing about the game. Due to an Indian summer, I found a suitable spot under a tree, placed my blanket on the ground and sat reading my book. My skin was very fair and the sun was surprisingly strong. I tried to watch the boys play but had no idea what a line out was or indeed how the game was scored. I watched in blissful ignorance.

Michael had been very welcoming and had in no way displayed the behaviour that the other teachers had described. He was surrounded by a group of misfits who followed him everywhere. Nathaniel Corby-Jones was a tall and lanky boy, who had outgrown his school uniform about three years ago. He was bespectacled and incredibly intelligent. Oliver Lockhart was the complete opposite. He was small rotund boy, had a mop of curly hair and couldn't string three words together. I believed he was intellectually redundant. Finally there was Timothy Grayson, a sporty, outgoing, good looking boy whom many of the younger boys looked up to. How they got together to form this seemingly tight group was a bit of a mystery to me.

It was on that afternoon, as sat under the shading tree that all four of them descended on me. They all sat down around me as if I was a mother telling a story. Nathan suggested that we take a picture.

"What on earth for?" I asked slightly suspicious.

"It's for the end of term newsletter. Tim is writing an article," said Oliver.

"Very well then."

Rather than arranging themselves like you may do for a traditional school photo they organised themselves into poses that you may see in Tatler magazine. Michael began to rearrange his hair. With one swift movement he brushed the hair from his face revealing his incredible beauty. I had to stop myself from just wanting to stare. Once the photo was over Oliver suggested that I take a photo of them. This time Michael stood apart from the group, staring into the distance as Oliver handed me the camera.

"Hey, Michael, you're not in a bloody fashion show," uttered Oliver "Bloody poser."

The afternoon wore on and finally Timothy, who looked incredibly bored, whispered something in Oliver's ear.

"May we go for a walk, Miss Kendall? Just around the grounds," asked Oliver.

"Well I don't see why not, but stay within the grounds please."

"Sure. Are you coming Michael? We are going for a walk".

The three boys looked at each other and looked like they had conspired this before they even sat with me. Michael, who was lying in the grass next to me, spoke directly to me.

"No. I'll stay and keep you company, Miss." The three boys left us alone.

"It's fine, Michael. I'm fine. You go ahead."

"They are so childish anyway. You do know they are going for a smoke?"

"I'm pretending I never heard that."

What happened next happened so quickly I didn't have time to think. Michael attempted to rise from the grass but instead fell in my direction and indeed on top of me.

"Michael. What are you doing?"

"Sorry Miss, Dead legs."

"Oh. No harm done." I brushed my skirt and rearranged my sitting position.

He then stared a long deep stare into my face and gently lifted his hand to remove a stray hair from my forehead. He paused before he spoke.

"You have beautiful hair Miss. My mother's hair was so coarse but yours is so soft."

I don't know what made me let him carry on. He was very gentle, more so than Robert. We kept eye contact for a few seconds before I picked up my book and began to read. He lay at my feet like a puppy, sucking on a blade of grass.

"What does your boyfriend do?"

"He is a concert pianist."

"Where did you meet?"

"After a concert he gave we both tried to grab the same taxi. We shared it and we became a couple. You should hear him play, Michael: it is so passionate and exciting. He has this intense scowl on his face like the world would end if he stopped playing. After the final note he looks like he's been in a boxing ring."

"Is he older than you?"

"Yes, a lot but age is just a number, it shows how long you've been alive but has no bearing on how much you've lived."

"Surely living and being alive is the same thing."

"Just wait until you're a little older," I smiled.

Just then I heard the voice of a crow. Miss Simms was making her way towards me with three boys stuffed under her arms.

"Miss Kendall!" I pretended not to hear, "Miss Kendall!"

Miss Simms bustled up to where we sat and dumped the three boys practically in my lap.

"Miss Kendall, I found these boys wandering the school grounds. They say you gave them permission."

"Yes I did. I saw no harm in it."

"The boys are not allowed to stray."

"They are not dogs, Miss Simms."

"I've already told the boys...."

I butted in, "Yes I'm sure you have. Excuse us we must be getting back indoors."

Miss Simms would never call me 'Mary' throughout my time at Bramleigh. I wanted to call her Margaret so badly but I was saving it up for the right moment. The three boys walked on ahead leaving Michael with us both, much to the disgust of Miss Simms.

"Walk on boy," she barked at Michael.

I nodded to him and he grabbed the blanket and took my book from me. Miss Simms suddenly grabbed my arm and promptly issued me a warning.

"Be very careful, Miss Kendall. That boy is a menace."

"Why is everyone warning me about this boy?"

"He has a reputation. He has taken a real shine to you. He is trouble."

"Well thank you Miss Simms for enlightening me but I think I can form an opinion of my own thank you."

"You have heard about his mother I take it."

"Chad told me that she was dead."

"Not just dead Miss Kendall, she was murdered in their house; in the basement. It was all very suspicious. He will destroy you lass, just like he did his mother."

Miss Simms then bustled off to wherever she goes once we were inside. I could still hear her footsteps as she was climbing the stairs. I could only think that she was jealous of the relationship I had with the boys. But her warning for a short while perturbed me.

I received a letter from Robert the following day. As I had no morning classes I took my letter to the Garden to read:

"My dearest Mary,

Just a note to let you know how much I am missing you. It seems so long ago that we last talked to one another let alone be alone with each other. I hope that your mother is in good health and your brother is keeping up his wonderful paintings. I think he has a real talent there.

Our tour is almost complete. Chopin is always popular. We have had a few nights of ovations which have been very thrilling indeed. My favourite place was Venice. You would love Venice, Mary. The beautiful buildings; the food and of course the romantic atmosphere. I cannot wait until you are all mine. Mrs Robert Searle.

Well my love. Miss you, as always.

Robert"

I missed Robert terribly. I thought I had found my soul mate. Robert was 36, considerably older than I. He was rather old fashioned in the way he dressed and certainly in the way he behaved. I think I loved that quality from the day we met. I understand now that when you are young you look at everything differently. Everything is bigger, everything is better and you believe you will never fall in love like this again.

The rest of the day was uneventful. Michael's class worked hard. Our topic of discussion was of Hamlet's madness. Real or pre conceived. What followed was a lively debate. Times like these made me love being a teacher. That evening, my night off, Chad drove us to the cinema in the local town. It wasn't a modern cinema as it showed old black and white movies. It was nice to escape the school even if it was for just an evening.

On our return, I was preparing myself for bed when I heard a small knock at my door. It was Michael. He stood rigid, eyes wild and most noticeably he was barefoot.

"Michael, what on earth are you doing here?"

He remained still, staring at me as if he was afraid to break eye contact. "Do you feel unwell?" I tried to coax an answer from him. Instead he started shivering uncontrollably. "Come on in. Sit yourself down." He came in looking quite bewildered.

He paused over my armchair until I physically gently pushed him into it. I crouched down beside him and held his hand. He eyes became a little less afraid and just as he was about to speak, Miss Simms burst through my door.

"Miss Kendall. So there you are boy. Get back to bed immediately. Your friends aren't terribly loyal about your whereabouts are they? Move boy right now!" she demanded.

Michael rose to leave. I ignored Miss Simms, determined to find out what was wrong, "Is there something you need to tell me?" He stood up, released his hand from mine and looked straight into my eyes. He smiled a small half-hearted smile and then left the room. I rounded on Miss Simms.

"What gives you the right to come bursting in here?"

"You should not be entertaining at this time of night."

"Excuse me. Entertaining! I'm not some sort of harlot. He was upset he came to see me. How dare you, Miss Simms, accuse me of anything improper." I was livid but remained calm; I would not let her get the better of me.

"This is the third time this week he has gone walkabout like some roaming Don Juan. The Head will be hearing of this you mark my words."

"This is the only time he has come to me." I tried to appeal to her better nature but as Chad had warned me Miss Simms had no better nature. "He seems to trust me. I feel that is so important. If he has someone to trust perhaps we might found out why he behaves the way he does."

"Miss Kendall, I've been at this school longer than any other member of staff. I have known this boy for nearly seven years. He should not be at this school. He is only here because no-one else wants him."

"What about his relatives?"

"As I have already told you, Miss Kendall, his mother was murdered in their home. The boy apparently found her body. She had been strangled. And as for his father, I am not privy to that information; suffice to say it is not he who pays for his education here. Well anyway, good-night, sleep well." She turned sharply and left.

My mind was reeling; murdered mother, absent father. I was under no illusion that this boy was rightly disturbed after such traumatic events. Sleep well! Miss Simms surely was joking.

Things went from bad to worse over the next couple of days. I was incredibly excited about Robert coming to visit. There was nowhere to put him up in my rooms so we had a room booked at a local bed and breakfast. I was supposed to meet him at the station but there had been an emergency here. Michael had somehow put his fist through a window. There were shards of glass everywhere and somebody had to accompany the boy to the hospital. Chad was happy to drive us and I was frankly happy for his presence. On our return Robert, who had had to pay for a taxi to the school, was not impressed by my disappearance or the sombre welcome given by Miss Simms.

"I have been away, Mary, for three months, am I not important enough to warrant your presence?"

"Of course you are Robert, but there was an emergency here. I was on duty so I had to go. A boy was hurt."

He didn't let it stop there, "I just cannot understand, Mary. I am important. I deserve your attention. Is it too much to ask of you?"

"Please, Robert. This is just a small incident. I'm looking forward to being with you and hearing about your tour. Please remember though I'm needed for the boys here. I am genuinely pleased your here. Can we just put this behind us?"

I did not recognize the man standing before me. Robert, when I met him, was a kind man and generous in spirit. He pushed me into teaching here. He now seemed distant and selfish. I thought it might be the artistic temperament shinning through but it was a side of him I was beginning to dislike. Over the weekend we went on walks across the moors. We stopped in small pubs and had lunch and enjoyed our time together. He returned to York on Sunday evening.

We parted with words of love but I was having my doubts that we should be together forever.

CHAPTER THREE

Things at school managed to tick along nicely. Michael's behaviour seemed to be under control and thankfully it seemed Miss Simms was even giving me a wide birth. The next free weekend I caught the train to York to visit Robert. His family were there and that he wanted to show me off to them. Robert's father was a barrister and his mother a University lecturer. I still can't recall what subject she taught. Like all prospective daughters-in-law they both feigned interest in my ramblings while making up their minds up as to whether I was worthy to marry their ultra talented son. Robert always played the piano for them and I would dutifully sit beside him turning the pages.

This visit however I was far more distracted than usual. As I boarded the train I somehow really missed not being in the safety of school. Trips out of the grounds were very rare even to the village shops. I had gotten use to the remoteness and dependence of my life there.

Robert picked me up from the station and gave me the dutiful kiss on the cheek. Previously this used to upset me but that day I thought nothing of it and just expected it. His apartment had a wonderful view of the cathedral and the cleanliness of his place made me paranoid about making a mess. It seemed like a show home rather than a lived in home. Near the French windows was an incredibly beautiful Steinway piano. I always believed he loved that piano more than me.

After a couple of hours, arguing raised its ugly head. I had managed to get through dinner, and suffer the boredom of Robert's parents. It was during the recital that things really took a turn for the worst. I loved Chopin and he usually played a piece for me. That day however he took to some dramatic Beethoven. My sight reading and page turning were a little rusty.

"Mary, turn the page!" he barked at me.

"Sorry. I'm not familiar with this piece, Robert"

He only had to wait a couple of minutes before it happened again.

"For God's sake, Mary, keep up."

I was incredibly embarrassed as his parents looked on in disgust. How dare I ruin their son's performance? My fingers began to get hot and sweaty and my brain could not keep up with such intense music.

"Too late! Too late!"

His frustration got the better of him and in one sweep of his arm he knocked the entire music score onto the floor. "What has got into you Mary?" he roared at me.

I retaliated quicker than I ever thought I would. "You don't need the bloody music. You know it more than you know me. I'm not an excellent musician like you. I play for my enjoyment, to make me feel happy."

His parents were hovering by the door wanting to make a quick and painless exit. Robert went to show them out as I picked up the music off of the floor. I pulled myself together determined not to cry. As soon as I heard the front door slam I began to walk towards him.

"I'm sorry Robert. I'm just a little preoccupied at the moment."

"What's the matter? What is taking all your concentration?"

I needed to get some air; he would not want to hear about the school and those within it. I suggested we go for a walk. He agreed. His whole body was tense and I knew he was trying to control his anger. We walked to the local park. So there we sat on a bench in the dark, near a duck pond initially in silence. After a few minutes of silence he decided to remind me of all the things he had given me over the time we have been together.

"Don't I give you enough to command your attention? I take you to lunch and expensive dinners in the finest restaurants. Do I not give you my time and attention? I expect that to be at least reciprocated."

"I too have other commitments such as my school, the boys. They are important to me Robert, can you not see that?" I felt exasperated with constantly repeating myself about my work.

"You have changed so much, Mary?"

"No, Robert, people don't change; circumstances do. I am not the shy 19 year-old you first met. Due to this teaching post I've grown into a strong independent woman. I don't rely on you, Robert. My world will not collapse because you are not part of it."

"So you want to break up is that what you're saying?"

"No, Robert. I'm saying give me some space to enjoy my work and the space in which I can explore my thoughts and feelings. I am a little preoccupied with a boy in my tutor group. He has problems which for some reason he wants to share with me. I feel redundant in being able to provide comfort in some way. He has had a very sad life. I want to help him and sometimes he takes a little of my time, sometimes overlapping my time with you. The situation just requires a little compassion."

I approached him tentatively, and tip toed to kiss him. "I do love you, Robert."

"I know you do, Mary."

That was our parting conversation. I returned to the school that evening. It was late, and the silence was palpable. I crept past the boys' dormitories to reach my rooms. I had just washed and was getting in bed when I heard a knock at the door. I pulled my dressing gown on and grabbed the paraffin lamp next to my bed. I opened the door and there he stood. Michael. He stood silently and just stared wildly at me. It looked as if he had been in a fight. There was a cut along his forehead, the beginnings of a bruise around his eye and the knuckles on one hand were raw. His bottom lip was also bleeding. He was fully dressed in uniform apart from the feet which again were bare.

"Michael. What is the matter? Can you not sleep?"

"I'm so sorry, Miss. I didn't know where else to go," he whispered.

"Come in. You'll catch a cold."

I ushered him in and pointed to a chair. He seemed very jittery and looked constantly around the room.

"What happened to your face?"

"I fell." Of course I did not believe this response but thought better of questioning any further. I went into my bathroom to retrieve the small medical bag I kept for emergencies. As I returned to the room he had moved from the chair and stood staring out of the window.

"Here Michael, sit down and let me clean some of these wounds up. I'm afraid I'm no nurse so let me know if I'm hurting you okay." He nodded in understanding and a small whisper of thank you escaped from his lips.

"You should be in bed. Where have you been?" I continued to clean his cuts and bruises; he uttered no sound at all.

After what seemed like an agonising five minutes of silence he finally spoke, "I went for a walk Miss, in the grounds. I had a nightmare so I went out to clear my head. I don't want to go back to bed, Miss."

"I must let Miss Simms know where you are." I picked up the telephone and suddenly felt a hand hold my wrist tightly.

"Don't phone her," it seemed more of a command than request.

"You should not be here. I have to let someone where you are. Please let go of my wrist." He dropped his hand as suddenly as it appeared.

"That woman is evil. Please, please don't phone her." I was caught between putting this boy into the hands of the school tyrant or letting him stay with me, which would, of course be unethical and unprofessional.

"I thought you were different from the others. But you are not are you? You are just the same sad, pathetic woman like her." He was becoming more agitated and angrier. "Phone her then go on. I don't give a shit." He when gave a disturbing mocking laugh. "Phone the fucking bitch. Get me expelled."

"Why did you come to me? You turn up at my door in the middle of the night; you have cuts and bruises on your face. What do you want from me?" I asked bewildered.

"I thought you were different and would understand." He moved closer to the door, he looked at me in desperation. Whatever was bothering him was seemingly over-taking him.

"Understand what? Please let us talk. Let's sit shall we. Please." He moved back to me and sat down. His beautiful face seemed to crumble in front of me. I had to fight the urge to physically comfort him. When he spoke it was soft and inviting.

"I'm so tired. Please can I stay with you? I just can't go back there. They hate me, they all hate me!"

"You need to go back to your dormitory. You can't be here."

"I'll just die if I have to go back there," he said with such anguish.

I moved off the couch and knelt before him. I took his hands in mine and looked up at the innocent face bleating down at me.

"You can sleep in my bed. I'll take the chair. Come on let's get you in bed. It's late. If your dream is bad I'll be right here." I gently pressed my hand on the side of his face.

I took his hand and led him into my bedroom. He removed his clothes apart from a t-shirt and underwear. He then crawled over the covers into my side of the bed. He was asleep within minutes; for me sleep took much longer. What had I done?

That morning however would be far more memorable. I had fallen asleep in the comfy chair next to the bed.

I woke to find the sleeping child in my bed and Robert leaning over me.

"Robert, you scared me what are you doing here?"

"Mary, what on earth are you doing?" He was angry and the colour red.

"I was not expecting you."

"Evidently, I come to surprise you and I'm the one surprised!"

The sarcasm began to drip off his tongue.

I got up and pulled Robert into the sitting room, "Let me explain."

"You honestly have a believable explanation as to why a teenage boy is asleep in your bed? I'd like to hear it. Early morning detention perhaps?"

As he spoke Michael opened the door and stood rooted to the spot.

"Extracurricular activity was it? Why is this boy just staring at me?" I looked over and Michael seemed in a trance. There was no movement from him at all. I rushed over to him and managed to usher him back into the bedroom.

"Put on your clothes, Michael. I'll be with you in a minute." I gently caressed his face with one hand. I left him standing there unsure of what his reaction would be. Robert was sitting on the comfy chair with his head in his hands.

"You have really outdone yourself. I just cannot understand this. A boy! You would rather have a boy than me?"

"Robert. Please listen. Think of the boy."

"I want to bloody kill him."

"Don't be absurd. He came to me last night. He was very distressed. I was unable to calm him sufficiently to get him back to his dormitory. He slept in my bed. I was not with him. I slept in a chair next to him. I am deeply offended that you should think that I would take advantage of this child."

"He's nearly a man, Mary. I'm really concerned for you. You've been really distant with me. I so want to give you the life that you wish for. Tell me that you want that with me and not this boy."

I took his face in my hands, "I love you Robert. Please trust me on this. If you excuse me, I need to get ready."

"Are you asking me to leave?"

"Yes, Robert. Please leave."

As with most arguments with Robert I could not help the tears. I wiped what I could with the back of my hand and faced the small mirror near the door. As I swept my hair up I caught sight of Michael standing at the bedroom door. I quickly brushed the tears from my cheeks and turned round. Michael stood a few feet away, he moved quietly towards me. Before I could say anything, his arms were around me and I sobbed effortlessly into his chest.

The days went by and neither Michael nor I spoke of our innocent affair that night. We did however give a knowing smile when we passed in the corridor or while at lunch. I was living in a false sense of security, I know that now. Michael's behaviour had not changed and I would begin to wonder about my own sanity. It was my turn to have afternoon tea this week with my tutor group. If the weather was nice I would hold it outside but rain prevailed and I was forced to give it in my rooms instead.

Michael arrived with Oliver. Oliver had had to repeat a year owing to his intellect or rather lack of. Michael often tutored him. Oliver sat at my piano stabbing at the keys.

"Will you play us a tune, Miss?" he asked.

"A tune! A tune!" said Nathan, who had literally just arrived. "It's an opus or recital."

"Ooh listen to him!" replied Michael. "Move over Oliver. Let me play."

I watched him move towards the piano, force Oliver off the stool, onto the floor and change the seat to his liking. I was intrigued; he had never shown any interest in the piano or indeed in any music. He removed the music that I had been playing earlier and began to play. He played beautifully and with great dexterity.

I really enjoyed these informal gatherings as I had the chance to be freer with the boys and get to know them a little better. As I talked to Nathan and Oliver I heard my favourite Chopin piece being played behind me. It made me think of Robert, the Robert that I first met and the Robert who would play for me before we went to bed. I could feel the tears welling up but somehow managed to focus on the other two boys instead. Soon time was upon us and the boys needed to get back to their respective duties.

"Nathan, shouldn't you be supervising Chapman's form now?" laughed Oliver.

"Oh shit. Shit. Oh sorry Miss. Chapman will kill me if I'm not there. Thanks for the tea Miss. Well worth coming for even if I do get detention." He rushed out still with remnants of cake around his face.

"He's never there. It's a wonder they keep asking him."

"He'll keep asking him, Oliver, until he is there on time. It is responsibility boys. If he is not good at time keeping what will he be like when he becomes a doctor! I hope his patients have more patience," I grinned.

"Are you coming to the common room, Michael?" asked Oliver. Michael was still at the piano, and did not look up when addressed.

"No, you go ahead. I'll see you at supper."

"Thanks, Miss, for the tea."

We were finally alone. I could not describe the feeling that I had. I desperately wanted to hold him, to be part of him. He turned to look at me; it was if he knew what I was thinking. He smiled and then began to play individual notes.

"You play so beautifully Michael. I never knew you played."

"My mother taught me. She could have been really good if she hadn't........." He didn't complete the rest of the sentence but like Oliver began to stab the keys on the piano.

I tried to fill the silence and change track. "What do you want to do when you leave here, University? You're bright enough for Oxford or Cambridge." I saw his face change into a blank stare.

"My father could never afford it."

"There are scholarships and things like that. A talented boy like you..."

I was not prepared for the barrage of anger that he then spat at me. He slammed both his hands on the keyboard, "Why? Why? Why does everyone think they know what I should do when I leave this place?"

"I'm sorry Michael, it is because you are so.........."
I didn't get the chance to finish.

"Gifted, intelligent is that it? I haven't got anything. I'm stuck in this shit hole because my father hates me. My mother is dead. I've had four sets of foster parents. You have no idea of what it is like being me. None whatsoever."

I dared to push a bit further: "You do have talent, Michael."

"And you like the others would hate to see this go to waste. That bitch Simms and the Head would like to see the back of me. Nobody wants me to shame the school... 'Michael Moorcroft such a promising boy: failed miserably in his endeavours.' I don't want to be a Doctor or a cabinet minister. I just want," he found it difficult to finish, "I don't know but wherever my parents are now they are laughing their fucking heads off!"

"That is so not true Michael." I made my way over to him and ran my fingers through his hair. The hostility subsided and he went seemingly back to his normal self. The mood between us lightened and I felt more comfortable being with him.

He turned to face me, "Did you always want to teach?"

"Yes, I suppose I did."

"Why not music?"

"I never thought I was good enough."

"But your so talented," he smiled with a hint of sarcasm. "Will you teach me another Chopin piece?" he asked sweetly.

"I don't know if I'm up to that kind of teaching!"

"Please, Mary," he dared to call me and I liked it.

"Okay, move over then." I sat down next to him, our bodies almost touching. "Chopin is one of the romantics, so we must play the piece with immense passion. Your fingers should glide across the keys, like this." My hands lightly pressed the keys. "Okay your turn." He began to play but stopped suddenly. "You're doing fine." I gently pressed my hands down on his and led his hands across the keys. My spine began to tingle, my heart beating slightly faster. He turned his head towards me. His face was breathtaking. I wanted to touch this beauty. He looked at me, smiled and leant gently forward to place his lips on my neck. My body relaxed and I surrendered to his touch.

CHAPTER FOUR

That night, as what seemed by now as clockwork, I was called to the boys' dormitory by Oliver and Nathan. They stood at my door, eyes wide and incomprehensible as they tried to tell me what was going on. I quickly put my dressing gown and followed the boys. I was expecting to see chaos. From what the boys had told me, Michael was hysterical, screaming and shouting. All the other boys in the room were awoken. Some of them were visibly shaken and were hiding beneath their duvets.

However upon my arrival, there was no noise no disruption from Michael. He was sitting by the window, staring quietly into the distance. Despite the anxiety and distress of the other boys it was if nothing had taken place. I stayed until all boys were in bed and made my weary way back to my rooms, too tired and a little bemused.

That morning I was awoken by Margret. I had slept in.

"Miss Kendall. Miss Kendall!"

I opened the door, "Come in; I overslept."

"Busy night from what I hear."

I ignored her and continued to dress and present my hair.

"Need I remind you that the Moorcroft boy is to be reported for any bad behaviour? He wandered again last night. I heard you were involved in that." She relished in telling me, "You know he was found sitting naked in the library this morning by the caretaker. Typical of course; that boy is such an exhibitionist."

"What time was this Miss Simms?"

"Around 6 o'clock."

"I saw him at around two o clock. His roommates were very concerned about him."

"All the same, I'm not one to gossip," a faint smile came to my lips. "You heard about his mother. He's an evil child."

"Please stop there. I must get on. Is there something that you need to say to me?" I opened the door to show my annoyance.

"Yes, the Head would like you to see him at eleven this morning in his office."

"Thank you. Please leave now."

"Well I have never been treated like this before," she said disgusted.

Luckily as we both stood staring at each other the phone rang. It was Robert. Due to my lateness he would have to wait to talk. He was not best pleased. I promised I would ring him later. I quickly made my way to the Headmaster's office. I arrived; slightly flustered.

"Mary, come in come in. Drink?"

"No, no thank you."

"I take it Miss Simms filled you in about the Moorcroft boy." I nodded in response; not sure of how much he actually knew. "Ghastly business, you know with his mother. It was all very suspicious. They arrested his father you know. He remained a suspect for quite a while I believe."

"No, I knew nothing of that."

"Anyway I digress. I noticed the boy has taken a real shine to you. Do you have any theories that could enlighten us about his behaviour?"

"Well, considering his background that you have just described, it seems the boy must feel very much alone in the world. He could just need some attention. The other boys have parents, holidays, treats and the comfort of family. He has his group of friends of course but he spends a lot of time alone. I find him to be a gentle boy who perhaps needs careful handling. I'm not a professional and can only speak from my experiences. He's got problems but what teenager hasn't."

"We have a reputation to uphold here. I will do anything within my power to protect the good name of this school. A lot of the teaching staff cannot tolerate his behaviour anymore."

"Are you going to expel him?"

My heart missed a beat.

"Ah there's the rub. We cannot expel him. An anonymous benefactor pays for his education here. And well above the school fees I might add. You know his father, was a highly regarded Senior Partner in a top accountancy firm. He embezzled nearly two million pounds of the company money. He was sentenced to eight years in prison. Just an awful business."

He stood at the window with his back to me, smoking his pipe. "You can see why the cogs are grinding to a halt. We cannot have a demented adolescent making a mockery of our establishment."

"Surely, Headmaster, he isn't then being properly provided for here? He needs some sort of security or supervision."

"Yes well," he sighed. "Our good name, Mary. Our good name." He paused for a few minutes, "Ah tea!"

Tea, the great British resolve. That was obviously it. Conversation ended. He handed me a cup of tea and it was a good five minutes before he spoke again. "How are you liking our little school?"

"Well. I'm more comfortable with my surroundings now. I had no idea that the school was so self sufficient.

The dark took getting used to. The boys are great. Very hardworking." I quickly drank my tea and made my excuse to leave.

That evening I received a phone call. My mother had been taken ill. Edward needed looking after. He should have been placed in a group home when he reached 18. He could live a more independent life but my mother could not bear him being away from her. Edward would always stay with her. I loved my brother deeply. He had a sweet nature but looking after him is always time consuming and sometimes difficult. Chad offered to drive me to the station and I eventually reached home around midnight. Edward was up and fully awake. My mother fortunately had a mild bout of flu and needed just a few days to rest.

While at my mother's I eventually called Robert. I apologised for the brief and perhaps a little curt response when I answered the phone. He seemed to understand and we were able to share the time on the phone at ease. Of course I could not keep away from the school. Once off the phone with Robert, I immediately rang Chad. All was well. There had been no incidences with Michael. Or so I believed.

CHAPTER FIVE

Once back at school I felt happy and confident after my week away. Before I had even taken my bag up to my room, a junior boy ran up to me with a message. I was expected now at the Governors' meeting in the Headmaster's office. I quickly dumped my bag in my room and ran back down just entering the meeting just a few minutes after it had started. Two men and one lady were seated around the table. The Headmaster indicated for me to sit on the free chair. This certainly looked more official than some of the other meetings attended. I did wonder if it was me that was being discussed.

As I sat down, one of the men looked around the table and said, "We need to get rid of this boy. We cannot afford a scandal. What if this gets out? The press will have a field day. Jenkins' father writes for one of those dreadful, cheap papers. He'll run it onto the front page. We will have endless streams of journalists leaping out of bushes and God only knows what else."

I did not recognise this man but he seemed to be the leader of the group. The Headmaster looked at me, "Oh sorry, Mary. This is Dr Jessop," indicating the gentleman who just spoke." These are Councillors Derek Hawkins and Mrs Patricia Prothoroe. They are here to investigate the incident that occurred in your absence last week." Chad must have lied to me.

"Any chance of a settlement with the other boy's parents, Headmaster?"

"We don't know who the benefactor for this boy is Derek. We have never seen him. This boy has been here seven years and we have no name or address. We receive payment when it is due. End of story."

The lady sitting next to me, Patricia Prothoroe was eager to speak, as was I.

"We need a solicitor, Headmaster, and social services must be called to re- home him." I was completely in the dark as to what was going on here. Solicitors and social services? I made a meek hand gesture to participate in this conversation. The Headmaster nodded at me.

"Could someone tell me what has happened and why am I here at this meeting?"

"Of course," said the Headmaster, "a few days ago, Mary, your favourite pupil Michael Moorcroft punched a boy in the face. The boy suffered concussion from the blow and has extensive bruising over one side of his face. We could be facing police involvement and bloody lawyers. We cannot afford for this to leave the school. I have already talked to the injured boy's parents. They are happy to believe that it was a scrap between the two rather than an unprovoked assault."

"So, Headmaster," responded Councillor Hawkins, "we are putting this down to boyish prank. Are we all in agreement?" They all groaned which sounded like an agreed yes. "That should keep it all hush-hush. Where is the boy now?"

"Mary?" asked the Headmaster.

"He should be in games right now," I replied. "Excuse me Headmaster why am I here? You all seem to have made a decision?"

The Headmaster looked down at the boy's file and then pushed it in my direction. "You should read this Miss Kendall. We are counting on you to keep the boy on the straight and narrow. This," pointing towards the file, "should assist you more clearly."

"He is a jolly good batsman for the cricket team though! An asset to the school in that respect," added the Headmaster.

All three men sat around guffawing and muttering, "Excellent! Excellent!" to no-one in particular. I tried to engage Patricia in light conversation but was met with a cold stare from behind her half rimmed spectacles. The rest of the morning was uneventful.

That afternoon during a free period I took a mug of tea and sat outside in the small garden. It had been snowing overnight, it was cold but the carpet of snow looked beautiful. I opened the file: it was full of reports, medical, psychological and general social service reports. The first page contained the names of the foster carers Michael was sent to over seven years. What drew my attention was the length of time he spent with them. It read:

Foster Care placements for: **Michael Robert Moorcroft**

Date of Birth: **15 July 1987**

Place of Birth: **London**

  Mr and Mrs A Freeman (August 1998):

    length of stay: 4 days,

    reason for withdrawal: non compatible placement.

  Mr and Mrs R Cummings (August/September 1998):

    length of stay: 11 days,

    reason for withdrawal: non compatible placement

  Mr and Mrs J Romer (September 1998):

    length of stay: 9 days,

    reason for withdrawal: non compatible placement.

The final placement was with a Mr and Mrs S Hope. I smiled to myself thinking of the irony of name and his situation. This placement lasted seven years, but only incorporated the longer summer and Christmas holidays. He had remained at school for all other term holidays. Last summer however they refused to have him back. There was no indication of the reason for refusal. Other reports indicated that he showed aggressive behaviour with other children; a desire to remain alone; refusal to co-operate and numerous attempts at running away. He managed to hide out from his foster carers for three days.

These reports did nothing but confirm to me that Michael was an incredibly mixed up child but over time had developed coping strategies and great independence. I could not believe that any other child would have acted differently given the same circumstances.

That evening I received a phone call from Robert. He felt that he had jumped to conclusions about Michael and me and was trying desperately to apologise and make it up to me. I made myself listen to what he had to say but could not help feeling that he always assumed everything and jumped to conclusions. He assumed that I would marry him; he assumed that once we were married that I would no longer teach. He saw me with a pupil and suggested a relationship seen in a Fellini film. He was sweet and contrite but my feelings for him had sadly now changed. Interspersed with confused feelings for Robert I had developed confused strong feelings for Chad. Chad was slightly older than I but I cared greatly for him and felt a sense of security when he was around.

CHAPTER SIX

That night, I was called to the boys' dormitory again. Oliver had come to collect me.

"Miss, he is saying he did it!"

"Did what? What is happening?" I hurried along behind him, "Oliver?"

"Miss, please hurry."

"What is going on?

"We got back from prep. Michael hadn't gone. There was a chair, which had been thrown into the door. His book bag was empty and books thrown all over place. He just sat on the bed, rocking back and forth saying: 'I did it! I did it!'"

"Have you woken Miss Simms?"

"No, Michael says she's a witch or something."

"Don't be ridiculous. Go fetch her at once. You silly boy!"

I thought better of her and the Headmaster's involvement but I could not have dealt with this myself or so I thought. I arrived at the dorm; it felt and looked like nothing had happened. There was a tidy pile near the door of a broken chair and lamp. Michael was sitting on the window ledge completely calm. Could this have been a practical joke? It was rather silly if it was one. Miss Simms arrived in due course desperate to make something of it. I went over to Michael.

"Michael, are you okay?" I gently stroked the side of his face.

"I'm perfectly well, thank you. What are you doing here?" he said matter of factly.

"The boys told me you were upset."

"Do I look like I am upset?" he responded sarcastically.

Miss Simms was straight off, "Get to bed, all of you. You too Moorcroft. I've had enough of your nonsense."

As I moved towards the door, Oliver and Michael exchanged glances. It was unreadable. I made my way back to my room. I don't know if I was disappointed: disappointed that I could not comfort him; or that he didn't want me to. The last thing I heard as I left had been "You're a fucking psycho, Moorcroft." I could not sleep so started marking term papers.

As I entered the common room next morning there was a buzz in the air that I hadn't felt since I arrived.

I assumed it was a birthday celebration or some other joyous occasion but this theory crashed as Miss Simms arrived. She had a triumphant look on her face. All questions were directed her.

"Where did you find him, Miss Simms?" asked Mr Chapman, intrigued.

"What is going on?" asked Chad, who made his way towards me.

"The Moorcroft boy. He was found sitting naked in the library by the caretaker."

Chad gave a stifled laugh. "Which section was he in Margaret, human anatomy?" I elbowed Chad in the ribs: "Sorry."

I had great trust in Chad and wanted to use him as a confidante. I cornered him at lunch, "Chad I must tell you something which you cannot share."

"Sure"

"I'm really serious, Chad."

"Okay, Mary. Sure. You can trust me."

"Last night I was called to Michael's dormitory. The boys were very distressed. They told me he had thrown his bag across the floor and threw a chair against the door. When I arrived it had been cleaned up and he was sitting there completely serene wondering what we were all on about. This is not the first time, Chad. I haven't told anyone else. I've been called to him several times."

"Mary, for Christ's sake what are you doing? I told you to leave him. How often have you?"

"That's not important." I tried to brush the comment off.

"Not important? He is not a kid to get too involved with. Leave him. Promise me, Mary. Promise me that you won't get too close to him." He physically shook my shoulder with his hand. I had never seen him like this.

"He's just a boy. He trusts me."

"Don't get involved. Period," he urged me. "Come on let's get a coffee. Talk about something else eh?" I could feel the prickle of tears behind my eyes. Chad did not know the half of it. I'd never spoken to anyone about our meetings together. The idea of telling him about Michael sleeping in my bed, kissing my neck and my sobbing into his chest were now out of the question. We went for a walk around the grounds. He put his arm around me. I felt somehow that a burden had been lifted just talking to him. As I made my way back to class I felt more buoyant and even managed a smile.

CHAPTER SEVEN

Within a matter of days, another incident was to put the school in chaos. Michael disappeared. The whole school was put on alert. Teams of boys headed out onto the moors with one of the masters to search. Before the police were involved we made a thorough search of the school and its grounds. We gathered in the staff room to be given an area to search. Not surprisingly Chad and I were given the basement. We were young and agile enough to cope with the small winding stairs. Basements are eerie at the best of times. Neither of us said anything about what we may find down there.

I followed Chad down the steps. There was no light so we had to find our way by torchlight. The schools generator was humming and every twenty seconds or so we would here a gush of water. We could hear the steps of the people above.

"This is so creepy, Chad." As I said this I grabbed his hand for reassurance.

"I know, just stay close. Who would want to hide here? His mother was killed in their basement. Why would he want to go down here?" He searched in the small areas hoping to find some clue as to Michael's whereabouts. The basement held no clues; only disappointment.

After fumbling away in the dark for ten minutes or so and seeing far too many mice for my liking we made our way back up to civilisation. We were to congregate back in the staff room. As we were the first back we grabbed a coffee and sat in the comfy armchairs near the fire. These were nearly always occupied by the older gentleman who needed an afternoon nap. It was quite a nice feeling being a bit naughty. Half an hour later everyone was back in the staffroom. The whole school had been searched. Nothing was found to give away his whereabouts. It was like he had just disappeared. The police and their search team were called and started to comb the moors. There were areas of the moors that could weather a fierce storm and these were searched first.

The school was full of police. The boys were shepherded into the main dining hall. A very soft spoken policewoman interviewed Chad and me in the staff room.

"Do you have any idea as to where Michael may have gone? What about friends or family?" she asked.

"Michael's mother has been dead seven years now. His father's whereabouts are unknown. He has three friends here at school, but quite superficially. He is really very much a loner. He has foster parents but they recently withdrew their foster parent status. He has just the school."

"He's very much an independent sort of boy, there is no question about that," added Chad. "It is not unusual for him to go missing. He has done it once before with his foster carers. He was 14. I think he was missing a couple of days. He is rather strange compared to the other kids."

"In what way?"

"Even though he is a loner, he commands the attention of his three friends who will do anything for him."

"Even lie?"

"Yes."

"What are the boys' names? I will talk to them next."

Chad gave the names of the boys. Chad put his arm around my waist in support.

"Thanks, we will obviously need to speak to them."

"I'll go and fetch them." Chad looked at me, dropped his arm, smiled at me and left the room.

"And what about staff here? Are you close to him?" she pressed.

"Yes, he is in my tutor group. He's a bright boy."

"Has anything happened to make him want to run away? An argument perhaps? Bad news?"

"As we have said he is very much alone. He has no-one outside school."

"Can you describe him for us? We will need a recent photo of him if you have one."

"Yes of course. The school secretary will have a photo on file. He's about 5 ft 10 possibly 11. Dark brown hair, relatively short. A fringe which he always flicks out the way. Brown eyes. Slim build. He has a finely chiselled jaw line which you can't miss. He is very striking to look at."

"Thank you. If you could get that photo for me that would be most helpful." She followed me to the school office.

Once the police were on the premises the seriousness of the situation was made more palpable. I was asked to take two constables up to the dormitory to look through Michael's belongings. Sometimes, they said, the smallest clue can provide enough to help them. The two constables looked around my age and fresh out of training. I could not help but want a more experienced officer. I felt rather awkward with their youth.

"If you could show us his clothes, suitcase or bags that would help a lot," one of them asked.

"Yes of course." I pulled his school trunk from under his bed and made my way through his sparse clothing. I looked in the small wardrobe beside his bed. "His school blazer is missing and a pair of pyjamas. All his shoes are here............ He must be barefoot." My voice cracked as I mentioned his shoes. I fought back the tears and carried on searching through his belongings. All his meagre collection of small personal possessions was still there. Bathroom items were still there. A wallet under his pillow was still full of cash.

The two constables wrote down everything in their little black books. "Thank you Miss. That's a real help." They left me sitting on his bed clutching a pair of his shoes. I went off duty after supper. I sat fully clothed in the bath and wept as if I could never weep again.

The next morning, I looked out of my window; the moors were still covered with a thick blanket of snow. The search had re-commenced. Realistically there was no way of searching all of the moors. They concentrated on areas known for rambling or where people had previously camped out. Every piece of paper, empty water bottle were picked up and taken back for investigation. As soon as it became dark the search was stopped and resumed the next day in daylight.

Even in the summer months, the moors were no place to get lost. One wrong turn and you would be wandering for days. As soon as I heard I tried not to panic but as time wore on my anxiety levels increased to an all time high. Outwardly and in company I just had to be a concerned teacher. Every time news came in was my pulse rate rose. I had visions of him lying in a ditch somewhere, falling into a bog, perhaps even starving and freezing to death.

I continuingly asked in the staff room for any news. I so wanted him back with me. I could not understand why Michael had not come to me before he decided to go. Had I done something to provoke or upset him? Only Chad knew of my real anxiety. He would give me updates when and if he had them. He had remained the loyal friend since day one.

The police were aware of Michael's history of his absconding and started to contact his foster parents. I have no record of what the outcome of these interviews was. As the days passed I taught and lived in a daze, clutching at hope that he would be found. As day three came sheer panic began to set in. The police continued their search with dogs. A helicopter was out scouting for any movement. In Hawksmoore, leaflets with his picture were posted around the village. No one came forward with any information regarding his sighting or whereabouts. The horror of what could happen to him became more intense. I was now positive that he would be found dead. I tried to carry on as normal, teaching my classes and undertaking my duties. I got very little sleep at night and began to wake early. I would sit staring out onto the desolate moors. It had been raining continually for the last four days. A night on the moor would be perilous, especially for a boy.

Day four came and went. The school carried on as normal. On the fifth day the Headmaster received a phone call from the local police station in Abbotswood, a small village around ten miles from the school. A boy in school uniform had been found wandering aimlessly. A member of the public had contacted the police concerned for his well being and as I suspected he was wearing no shoes. Chad and I were designated to go and pick him up. The search would be called off pending positive identification of him.

"At least they have found him alive, Mary," said Chad, a little too happy for my liking as he opened the car door for me.

"We don't even know it is him yet, Chad." All of my being however was praying that it was him.

"Oh come on Mary. How many other kids go wandering for five days in their school uniform? Most can't wait to take it off!" He was trying to make me smile. I wanted to see Michael's face before I smiled.

We drove into Abbotswood and parked in the police station car park. "Shall I come with you?" said Chad getting out of the car.

"Please." I needed his support especially now.

We walked up to the front desk and a burly looking police sergeant loomed over the desk.

"Hello, we received a call about a missing boy. We think he may be one of ours. We are from Bramleigh School near Hawksmoore."

"Oh yes, Miss. Strange lad that one. Found him just wandering aimlessly. A member of the public alerted us. We found him barefoot. He is wearing his school blazer. We recognised the school badge, of course, when we bought him in. He is very dishevelled wearing his pyjama bottoms." He turned to the constable standing behind him, "Go get the boy constable; these folks are here for him."

Chad and I were taken to a small interview room to wait.

"I'm afraid he has not spoken one word since we picked him up. Not even his name." said the constable.

Michael was led in by two constables. He was gently pushed into a chair. He looked pale and tired. His eyes stared ahead, unblinking. His clothes were dirty and torn. I looked down and his feet were bloodied. I stood up and moved towards him. I crouched down in front of him.

"Where were you Michael? We have been so worried about you.....Are you hurt?"

I was expecting silence from him but instead he raised his head and looked into my eyes.

"I went for a walk; just for a walk." He was completely defensive. "Am I not allowed to go out for a walk?"

"Yes Michael, but you've been gone five days. I was very worried and scared that something had happened to you. But it's okay Michael. You're safe now. That's all that matters."

"Let's get back to school shall we?" said Chad, opening the door.

As he stood up I noticed that there was a line of dried blood streaking down his arm. I pushed up his sleeve. There was a nasty gash on his elbow raw and full of mud. One of the constables leant down near my ear.

"He's got a nasty gash there. He refused to be seen by the doctor here. It looks like he fell. Not too bright is he?"

"Thank you, Officer. Is there anything we need to do here?" I was annoyed at their glibness.

"No, Miss. Just keep him out of trouble. We will liaise with the search team, confirming his identity and that he is now been found and is back with you. They may want to speak to again."

Chad gathered us together, "Okay folks let's get back to school." We drove in silence and reached the school at supper time. Miss Simms was waiting for us at the school entrance. Her arms were crossed underneath her rather large chest. Her face looked like thunder. We had literally just walked through the door when she barked orders at us.

"Right lad, go and get changed," she ordered.

"Miss Simms, I think he needs to be settled first. He needs to get out of these damp clothes before he gets a chill."

"The Head has asked me to collect a meal for Moorcroft and ensure he gets to bed. You are no longer required Miss Kendall." I felt Chad's firm hand on my arm and his head tilt towards the dining room. "The Headmaster will speak to him first thing in the morning."

We left Michael with Miss Simms. As he climbed the stairs, I could hear him whisper, "Thank you Mary." For the first time in days I gave a genuine smile.

I followed Chad into dinner, I was so tired and not particularly hungry.

"You need to eat too," said Chad pulling me into the Hall.

"You seem much happier, Mary," said Chad, pulling out my chair.

"Yes, I do. Thanks, Chad, I appreciate your support." I felt such relief that Michael was back safely. I was slightly put out that Miss Simms took over on our return from the station but I didn't let that ruin the moment. Dinner was underway when Miss Simms came rushing up to the Headmaster and whispered into his ear.

"Miss Kendall," he called, "I need to see you immediately. In the corridor please."

"Yes of course Headmaster." I pushed out my chair and followed him into the corridor where Miss Simms was also waiting.

"Please tell Miss Kendall what you told me Miss Simms," said the Headmaster looking very concerned.

"Well, Miss Kendall. After you returned I took Moorcroft up to the bathroom for a wash. His clothes are filthy. He is full of mud and grime. I asked him to remove his clothes. I ran a bath for him. The smell was awful Headmaster. I'm sure you would agree Miss Kendall. He refused to remove his clothes. He just screamed whenever I touched him."

"Screamed?" I asked astonished.

"Yes, screamed at me; an ear piercing scream. I went to help him remove his shirt and he bit me. Yes, he bit me, Headmaster."

"I find that very hard to believe, Miss Simms."

"Are you calling me a liar Miss Kendall?" she shot an angry look at me.

"No. I'm just saying that perhaps he is in pain or simply is embarrassed to. He is 17 not 10 years old. He is not particularly a demonstrative boy; perhaps he needed someone he trusts that's all."

"Miss Kendall, Miss Simms has worked with this boy for seven years," said the Headmaster, "I want you to go with Miss Simms, see what you can do."

"Of course, Headmaster."

I followed Miss Simms up to the boys' dormitory. Michael was sitting hunched over on his bed looking despondent.

"Hello Michael." I crouched down in front of him and brushed the hair away from his eyes with my hand. "You are really damp and dirty; you need to wash. You can't stay like this, it will be so uncomfortable. You are still wet through. Come, please. Miss Simms, please fetch some towels."

I put my arms under his arms, gently lifted him of the bed and led him by hand into the bathroom. "Let's get this shirt off, shall we?" His hands never left his sides. He stood still and silent. I reached up to undo his buttons, when Miss Simms came in with a towel. Suddenly he closed his eyes and gave a full throated scream.

"Get out. Stay away from me, you bitch, get out." He screwed up his eyes and then covered his face with his hands.

"Miss Simms, you should go and leave him to me. Please. Just go."

She stomped out angrily and very loudly, "The Head will be hearing about this."

I didn't care. His breathing was fast and his eyes wild so I gently lifted my hand and managed to unbutton his shirt. At first he flinched but made no sound and let me continue. As I opened his shirt I suddenly felt sick. I swallowed visibly. His young, bare chest was covered in red scars. Some were fresh, some deep and some superficial. I looked straight at him. Again he remained silent.

"Michael, please talk to me." Not even a nod of the head. I continued to remove his pyjama bottoms. He let me help him into the bath. His nudity didn't bother me. It didn't seem to bother him. I'd had to help bathe Edward in the past. Michael's body was pale, skinny and so terribly young. I took a deep breath. I grabbed a soft sponge and very gently began to wash him. The water was hot; I could feel his body relax under my touch. Soon his cold body became warm. I carefully poured a jug of water over his head and tenderly ran my fingers through his soapy hair. He began to smell sweet. I very softly cleaned around the wounds on his chest. He did not flinch when I touched those that were still raw. "There, do you feel a little better now?" He nodded slightly and stood up. The water must have been too hot as he swayed slightly as he stepped out of the bath. I held him for a moment until he was steady on his feet. I towel dried his body and hair and pulled him into his pyjamas. He silently wandered into the dormitory and sat on his bed. He looked completely dejected.

"Get into bed sweetheart." He leaned back and I gently lifted his legs under the covers. I sat on the bed near his head and stroked his hair until he fell asleep. I felt a feeling of unusual contentment. I wanted to stay longer just to watch him sleep. Miss Simms arrived as he had dropped off.

"The Headmaster is expecting you Miss Kendall!" she said flatly.

"Thank you Miss Simms, I'll be right there." She waddled out of the room. I stood up and softly stroked his hair and then left.

The Headmaster was waiting impatiently in his office for my return.

"Well?"

"He's asleep now. The police found him wandering aimlessly in Abbotswood."

"How the hell did he get there? It is at least ten or so miles from here."

"He hasn't spoken as to why he was there, to me or the police. At the police station he was completely mute.

I managed to bathe him just now. He has excessive scarring on his chest. I have no idea as to how they got there. He refused to see the police doctor. I would like one sent for in the morning. This boy is unwell, Headmaster."

I was reminded of my brother; he didn't make a sound until he was about six years old. He is practically mute. He was born deaf and all of us learned sign language. My mother and father did their best with him through his teenage years but this was extremely traumatic for Edward. We were offered a care home from social services to enable more independent life. My parents refused. Now my mother looks after him by herself.

"You say these wounds are recent? He did punch his hand through a window, Mary; this boy is a born manipulator. I do not believe his stories. I'll make my decision as to what to do with him in the morning. For God's sake keep him out of trouble until then."

"Yes, but what about the scarring? Surely we can't ignore them. We can't neglect our duty."

"I am very aware of our duty Miss Kendall. I trust you to remember that. Have Miss Simms look at them in the morning and talk to his friends will you. See if you can find out what he has been doing on his little outings. Wasting police time like that and returning with such arrogance."

"Good night then, Headmaster." I left his office feeling utterly defeated and made my way to bed.

CHAPTER EIGHT

That same night I received a visit from Nathan and Oliver. It was very late. I assumed there was a problem with Michael. There was a timid knock on my door.

"Please Miss, we need to talk to you."

"Who is it?" I called from my bedroom. I got out of bed and put my dressing gown on.

"Nathan and Oliver, Miss."

I opened the door and found the two boys huddled together. "What are earth do you want boys? It is so late. Is something wrong with Michael?"

"Yes and no, Miss," said Oliver shuffling his feet.

"Come in then, sit yourselves down." The small light from the paraffin light always made the room seem much smaller. The two boys sat close to each other on the sofa, each making subtle eye contact every few seconds. Both looked like they were frightened to be here.

"So what is it boys?"

Nathan looked at Oliver and gave a firm nod. Obviously to indicate that it was okay to talk.

"We know where Michael went when he disappeared. We......" Oliver paused, visibly upset and Nathan took over the story telling. "We lied about him being in bed at lights out, the day before he was reported missing. He said he would kill us if we told anyone. When the night prefect gave the report to Miss Simms he had already left the grounds." He bit his bottom lip, waiting for my response.

"Oh my God! We have had a major search by the police. Nearly 100 people were involved in finding him. You stupid, stupid boys."

"Where did he go Nathan?"

"He's going to kill us, Miss. We swore we would not say anything," said Oliver beginning to panic.

"Just tell me what you know." I tried to keep my temper in check. It could not have been easy coming to tell me. "Please continue."

Nathan fidgeted in his seat and wiped the tears that were now streaming down his face on his pyjama sleeve. "You know the clear water stream not far from here on the moors?" I nodded, Robert and I often walked there. "He goes there."

Oliver took over, "He removes his clothes Miss......kneels in the water and......says a prayer to wash his sins away."

Another long pause before he spoke again, Nathan remained silent with his head buried in his hands. "He takes a knife with him; he stole it from the kitchen. He makes a mark on his chest to signify each sin. We saw him Miss, we followed him."

I was completely shocked and quite nauseous at the thought. "How often does he do this? Is it always the same?"

"Yes"

"When did he start doing this?"

"Since the first year. We never found out until last year. He never changes his shirt in front of us, not even for games. We were curious as to where he got to. We always lied to the night prefect that he was always present at lights out."

"And the bare feet?"

"Jesus."

"Jesus?" I didn't understand what they were talking about.

"He believes he is Jesus, Miss."

I could not believe what I was hearing. I didn't know how to process this information. "What do you mean he thinks he is Jesus?"

"We are not exactly sure, Miss. He thinks that he is the saviour of the world."

"Does anyone else know about this?"

"We are not sure, Miss." Both boys looked ashamed.

"And you didn't think to tell anyone?" They both shook their heads in shame. "Is there anything else you need to tell me?"

Oliver looked at Nathan, "There is a woman he meets just outside the grounds. We have seen her but we haven't met her or anything."

"Can you describe her?"

"No, Miss. She sits in the car waiting for him."

"Okay, back to bed you two. I'll have to speak to the Head in the morning. This is very serious, you know that don't you?" Both nodded then left the room. My head was spinning. Deliberately harming himself and who was this woman he met with? I took myself back to bed, but sleep was not forthcoming.

Chapter Nine

My first port of call in the morning was to see the Head-master. He was not in the best of moods.

"I've just been on the phone with the police; trying to sort out this terrible debacle, wasting police time."

"Headmaster, I may be able to shed some light …." he didn't allow me to finish.

"This boy is driving me to distraction. What with his not washing; wandering around the school naked. He will be kept in sick bay with Miss Simms from now on. This I hope will curb the wanderings."

"Please listen to me. Oliver and Nathan came to me last night. They knew where Michael had gone. They were afraid to say anything."

I could feel that he was beginning to boil. "Please continue Miss Kendall."

"Michael believes, according to the boys, that he is Jesus," I said very seriously. "He goes to the clear water stream to cleanse his sins." I took a deep breath waiting for his response.

"Don't be ridiculous; I don't believe a word of it."

"The boys were afraid of him. Surely we must do something. Please, Headmaster, let me phone for a doctor or at least someone for him to talk to."

"Very well, Miss Kendall, you can phone for a doctor."

"Thank you." I felt a huge weight being lifted from my shoulders. I was finally allowed to do something to help him.

A doctor arrived around lunch time. But my hope was short lived. Michael had refused to speak to him. Even my presence did not help. He was able to look at his scarred chest but apart from the physical injuries which he could treat, there was nothing else he could do. I felt nothing but disappointment. I made my way back to the staffroom not knowing what Michael's reaction would be. I saw Chad and sadly made my way to him.

"They are doing nothing, Chad."

"Mary, he's been like this for a long time. What did you expect? You do far too much for that boy."

"I expected to be listened to, Chad. That boy is in pain and I going to help him if it kills me." I got up abruptly and left the room.

I walked slowly to the classroom and panicked. What would he be thinking? I very soon found out. He looked up, smoothly ran his fingers through his hair and gave me the sweetest smile. I felt better already. The atmosphere with the other boys however was slightly tense. Did Michael know that they came to me that night and exposed his world? I could not tell.

I sat down beside Chad at lunchtime. "He looks a lot better today; seems he's back to normal, well whatever is normal for him," he smiled. I watched how Michael manoeuvred his way around his friends and how calming it was for me to watch his behaviour.

Robert rang me at lunchtime and asked me out to lunch at Suzie's Tea House the next day; a quaint little cafe in Hawksmoore. I arranged to meet Robert there at 12.30. He was punctual of course.

"Robert." I kissed him on the cheek and showed my best smile.

"Mary, I've bought you these," he held out a bunch of lilies, "your favourite flowers."

"Oh thank you so much. How are rehearsals coming along?" He was rehearsing for a recital in Leeds.

"Great. It always takes a couple of days for everything to gel. What about you? Are you still chasing after naughty boys?" I did not smile. I did not laugh. "Oh come on Mary; that was funny."

"We have had a few problems but things have settled down now." We ordered two teas and began to drink in an awkward silence.

The door bell rang and I looked up to see Michael accompanied by what could only be described as a mature woman. Michael was dressed immaculately, the woman also. She must have been the woman the boys were talking about. I watched them as they sat at a table near the window, holding hands. She kept looking around and then whispering in his ear. I could not stop staring. Who was this woman? They were lost in conversation, I was lost in theirs.

"Mary!"

I suddenly looked at Robert, "I'm so sorry."

"Mary, I know my behaviour hasn't been great for the last few months, I've been under a lot of stress. I want to make it up to you. Please give me that chance. I love you, I need you. You belong to me."

"That is where you are wrong Robert. I belong to no-one." I looked into his sad face. I think he knew the inevitable. "You love the piano; you love your music. You love the idea of me. Not me. You need someone who can share your passion for music." Out the corner of my eye I could see, and eventually hear, the heated discussion between Michael and his lady friend. Michael was angrily pulling at her wrist.

"Let go of me, Mike." I had never heard anyone call him Mike before.

"You will do as I say," he responded to her.

A timid waitress moved towards them asking if she could do anything. The whole room was now staring at them.

In swift movement Michael was out of the door leaving the woman alone at the table. Casually the woman got out her newspaper, ordered a coffee from the waitress and carried on as if nothing had happened. "Who was that woman?" I kept asking myself. Only he would have the answer to that question.

I was feeling slightly faint, "Can we get back to the school Robert; I'm not feeling well." He nodded. As I stood up my legs gave way beneath me. Robert caught me and helped me towards his car parked outside. I felt such a fool. In no time at all Robert had carried me from the car to my rooms.

"Do you want a doctor, Mary?"

"No, I'll be fine thank you. I'm just a little hot I think."

"Still I think I should call..."

"No, Robert. Thank you, I will be fine." I motioned to him to sit on my bed. "Robert, I think you know what I 'm going to say. I think it's time we said goodbye to each other." I pulled off the engagement ring. "Here take this back. I'm sorry Robert but we were not meant to be together."

"It is that boy isn't it?"

"This is exactly why our relationship must end. He is no more than a boy; one of my pupils. That accusation can cost me my job. You have your music. I have my school and the boys."

"Please don't do this to me," he leant forward and took my hand. "I love you."

"I'm sorry Robert." I pulled my hand away. "You're a very talented man. I hope you will find someone deserving of you."

He stood up, I could tell that he was fighting back tears but would never be a man and let them flow. He kissed my forehead and slowly walked to the door.

He turned to me, "Goodbye Mary."

"Goodbye Robert."

As soon as he had left I felt the prickling tears behind my eyes began to flow. I didn't really understand what I was crying for: the loss of the friendship and the relationship; my hidden feelings for Michael; the friendship that I had with Chad. I just knew that something life altering had happened.

Without knocking Miss Simms barged through my door. "Your fiancée wanted me to sit with you."

"Oh, Miss Simms, I feel much better. That won't be necessary."

"Oh." She turned on her heels and noisy stamped her way downstairs.

I had had the afternoon off so caught up on my correspondence. I would inform my mother of my single status the next time I was home. She had enough to think about with Edward. Just after 11 pm I heard a small knock at my door. I thought it may be Chad as he said he would pop by and see me.

"Come in, the door is unlocked."

The door pushed open. It was not Chad who had come to see me but Michael.

"Michael! I thought you were someone else. What are you doing here? Does Miss Simms know you are here?"

"I've come to see you, Mary," he said softly.

He walked towards me, confident and smiling. Even in the dimness of the light I could see his perfect face. It took my breath away.

He motioned to sit down on the bed. "May I?" I nodded.

He sat down on the bed near to my chest. I tentatively moved my shaking body towards his. I looked into his eyes; they were dark brown; his long eyelashes encasing their beauty. I opened my arms to him and embraced his slender body. I held him close afraid to let go. He smelled so sweet. We both leaned back on the bed. I pulled his body closer to me. As we lay there he began to play with strands of my hair. He held my face with both his hands and I surrendered to his tender kiss.

CHAPTER TEN

A few days later, Michael failed to turn up to class. This was very unusual. I made my way to his dormitory. He sat transfixed, staring into a corner of the room.

"Michael, you didn't attend class today. Are you okay?" He gave his usual response: silence.

I tried again, "Michael, did you hear me?"

"I heard you," he snapped.

"Well, you need to get to class now."

"I can't." He kept his eyes fixed on the corner.

"What do you mean, 'You can't?'"

"She wants me to stay with her."

"Who does?"

"My mother of course."

I was very concerned and confused. "Your mother is dead Michael."

"I know," he barked at me, "she told me she wished me to stay with her, especially today." He was holding a photo of her. "So no-one can hurt her again. I wish to stay with her."

"I'm sorry about your mother but there is no-one here but you and me here. It has been seven years since she passed away Michael."

"She is in the corner, can you not see her?" He pointed to the corner. "She is standing right there. She likes you, Mary."

"Listen to me. I understand you are upset that she died."

"She didn't die, Mary. She is here."

"No, Michael, she is not." I tried to be firm but also caring.

"Stop lying, Mary? How could you? Get out of here you lying bitch. Get out."

I rushed out; tears streaming down my face. I rounded the corner and came face to face with Chad.

"Hey! What is the matter? Are you okay, Mary?" He shook me until I answered.

"I'm losing my mind, Chad."

"It can't be that bad surely?" He tried to make me smile. "Come let's get a coffee and you can tell Chad all about it."

We wandered into the staffroom. Thankfully it was quite empty. We sat near the fire.

"What is it?"

"Michael."

"Ah everyone is talking about Moorcroft."

"He missed my class this morning. I went to find him. He was staring at something in the corner of the room. He said he wanted to stay in his room because his mother wanted him to. He was pointing at nothing, Chad."

"Hey the kid's lost his mom. It is only natural to grieve on the day she died. You said it yourself: the kid has no-one. It must be real hard for him."

"I cannot get the image of a child weeping over his mother's dead body out of my mind."

"It is hard, Mary. We all do now that you know, even the Head. He's been very strange since we have had him here. When he first arrived he stayed in a room next to Margaret. He had dreadful nightmares. He would scream a lot. He needed to be sedated most nights. It has been hard for staff to get close to him. You are probably the first person throughout his stay here to get remotely close to him. You are doing a real nice job with him. I know I get on your nerves about you and him but you've probably saved him from a lot more misery. What about that doctor who saw him?"

"He says he is physically fine."

"What about a shrink?"

"He is not crazy, Chad."

"Maybe not but there is no denying that he's got problems."

The bell rang for our next lesson.

"Look, Mary, I'll keep an eye on him okay?"

"Thanks, Chad. You are so wonderful," I gushed.

"I know; I know! Don't let it get around," he laughed.

The afternoon was taken up by another Governors' meeting. I was asked to be there and strangely so was Miss Simms. The room this time had more than three governors. We all took our seats and silence was called for.

"It has been bought to my attention that several older boys are going into the village at lunchtime mainly Suzy's tea house. This place is strictly forbidden; Rule breaking will result in immediate suspension. Miss Simms will be dealing with this with frequent trips there.

"That bloody boy again," said a balding man next to the Headmaster.

"As of yet I have yet to hear his name being mentioned but his friends are making a habit of it. They are exercising their free time with immense alacrity."

"What is the problem there Headmaster?" asked the only female governor.

"It is a place where ladies like to frequent."

"As for ladies do you mean..."

"So I am told," replied the Headmaster.

"Excuse me Headmaster, I go there frequently and have yet to see that aspect on their premises," I said amused and quite shocked at the seriousness of their allegations.

"Surely, Headmaster, the integration of girls should be encouraged. Otherwise these boys will leave without any interaction with woman. I'm sure Miss Kendall will agree with me. The ladies you mention I'm sure are just local girls. Freedom of expression surely must be encouraged."

"They will have plenty of time for women once they leave here," said the Headmaster. "So the first thing on the agenda is of course the Moorcroft boy."

"When is he going to be expelled, Headmaster?" demanded Miss Simms.

"Miss Simms, I've heard your views and that of the other board members and it is very clear he is causing immense tension and upset within the school. We must tread cautiously. He is not the only one to have caused problems at this school and he won't be the last. We must keep our chins up," replied the Headmaster.

"It is to do with money of course," ranted Miss Simms.

"Please, this is not a time for that discussion." Now the floor opened to what would be a lively debate.

"He is disruptive, abusive and a bad influence on the other boys. He is a rotten apple. Let social services have him." They were general guffaws and nodding in agreement.

I could not help but to speak. "Will you just listen to each other? He is also a bright boy with enormous potential. His background is what the problem is. He has no parents; no guiding hand. With the right handling he can be a hardworking caring young man."

"We can't allow those who have emotional problems to stay here."

"Why? There is something wrong here and you are not doing anything about it. If you're not going to expel him then we have a duty to care for him."

"What do you suggest, Miss Kendall?" asked the female governor.

"Get someone in to come and talk with him....."

"Miss Kendall, this is a public school, not a therapy centre for wayward adolescents. If there is no other business we will leave it there."

Chapter Eleven

The next few days passed quietly and, although extremely quiet, Michael seemed to be recovering from his ordeal. The Headmaster over the next few days would be looking into his disappearance and making a decision as to where Michael would be sent, if anywhere at all. He only had a year left and I had my fingers crossed that the Headmaster would give a reprieve allowing him to finish his studies with us.

Chad seemed very excited as I walked into the common room at break time. He seemed very eager to talk to me.

"Mary, how about dinner in town this Saturday? I know of a little restaurant we could go to."

I was still a little reluctant to share more personal details and indeed my feelings with Chad. He was very easy to talk to and seemed completely trustworthy but it seemed unfair to burden him with my neurosis.

"Oh, that would be lovely Chad, thank you." It would be nice to get away from the school for a few hours. After Michael's escapade the school was on alert for more disruptive behaviour. Michael was now under the auspices of Miss Simms. Every half hour she would note down Michael's whereabouts. At bedtime he slept in sick bay, next to her rooms so she could hear any movement. I found it to be too intrusive but my opinions were always listened to and then promptly discounted.

Saturday was soon upon us and Chad and I made it into Hawksmoore that evening. The restaurant was small and cosy and we were given a quiet table by the window. Something other than school food was also very welcome.

"How long have you lived in England, Chad?" I asked for openers. Both of us seemed a little nervous being together out of school.

"Since childhood. None of us have got a British accent though. I have a brother and two sisters. Quite a collection of us. I went to Durham University and then came here after teacher training. I like the smallness of the school. You can get involved more and the size of class is smaller and so much easier to teach. I've been at Bramleigh for 3 years now. I would not go anywhere else. I also get a chance to organise the sports. Mr Channing can only look on, at 53 years young; while I, being the agile guy that I am, can actually participate." We both laughed. We were the only two staff members under 30.

"What about your brother, Mary?" he asked.

"Well, he's my twin. I think I've told you that. Edward is autistic but also deaf. It's very difficult for outsiders to communicate with him. My mother and I use sign language. Sadly he is not as independent as we hoped he would he. We have been offered a group home but my mother refuses to send him away from her. I am needed at home when she is unwell because he relies on stability and routine. He can get hysterical if things are out of place. But I love him so much Chad. I couldn't be a whole human being without him. I've never experienced the twin connection, whatever that is, with him. He lives in his own world in which we are not invited. It would collapse if Mother and I were not there. My father died of pancreatic cancer last year. Even through the last months he still fiercely devoted to Edward. He was such a good man my father. I miss him a lot.

"Edward reminds me of Michael in so many ways. So vulnerable but he has an inner strength which allows them to be safe. Edward is also beautiful to look at. He would have been a real ladies' man. My mother often looks up to God and demands why her boy has been inflicted by such a horrible illness if he was given such beautiful features. My mother is a Catholic. She spends a lot of time confessing and praying." I smiled when I said it. "I should not be so uncharitable but that is just the way she is."

"You seem very protective of him; Michael that is. He isn't your brother. That kid has a resilience that I never encountered before. I don't want to see you hurt. I think you may have been misguided."

I smiled at him. "I'm a big girl, Chad. I can look after myself. But thanks for caring so much. I do appreciate and value what you say."

I felt unease for a few minutes, sensing that he wanted to say something to me.

"What's up Chad? You've being dying to ask me something since we arrived. What is it?"

He took a deep breath, smiled a nervous smile, "Mary, I'm so much happier since you have come to teach at Bramleigh. I always felt rather awkward and given that Miss Simms was the only female in the building, I felt somewhat redundant in the ladies' department. What I'm trying to say Mary is that I'm very attracted to you..."

I reached my hand out and touched the side of his face, "Oh Chad, please don't say things like that. I love you as a good friend. Someone I can trust and someone who makes me laugh. I don't think we should complicate things."

"I love you Mary," he pleaded. He took my right hand and gently kissed it.

"Chad, I'm only coming to terms with losing Robert. Although that breakup was easier than I thought I still do love him. Part of me still yearns for him and the sensible part of me just can't wait to let go. Chad, let's just leave things as they are and see what happens in the future. I couldn't imagine being here without you to." I had never before studied his face. He had boyish features, striking blue eyes which always seemed glow and a smile so huge and genuine.

"I'm sorry I just speak as I find. It's an American thing." He laughed but behind his big blue eyes I could see a great sadness. I leaned over the table took his face in mine and kissed him on the forehead. After a few minutes of uncomfortable silence, we began chatting again. There may have been a hint of embarrassment on both sides.

The meal was excellent, so much better than food cooked for one hundred at the school. Like a gentleman Chad paid despite my protestations. We left the restaurant around half past ten in enough time to drive back to school and without being locked out. We were all set to go when Chad's car decided to give up on us.

"Darn it," he cursed, "out of petrol. I knew I should have filled when I was in town last. Damn; Damn; Damn." He thrust his hands in his hair, pulling whatever hairs he could; "I'm so sorry, Mary."

"These things can't be helped, we can order a taxi." He handed over his phone and in no time a taxi had arrived. Chad was worried about leaving his car, what with no roof. He reluctantly got in the taxi intending to return the next morning with a can of petrol. By now it was 11.15 we had missed the curfew at school and would have to wake Miss Simms to let us in.

"It's alright Mary. I'll protect you from the forces of evil," laughed Chad. I couldn't help but smile.

"She's going to be livid, Chad."

"Oh well," he shrugged.

The taxi pulled up at around 11.45. I was tired now and desperately needed my bed. Chad rang the bell which would ring in Miss Simms' room. We counted how long it would be before she marched to chastise us.

"What time do you call this?" she bellowed, opening the front door.

"I believe it is 11.51 Margaret," said Chad sarcastically. "Excuse us we must get to our rooms now." He took my hand and pushed past us.

"The Head will be hearing about this." She waddled back to her rooms.

Chad grabbed paraffin light and escorted me up to my rooms. "Thank you, Chad. I had a lovely time."

"So did I, Mary. Let's do it again some time." He leant forward kissed my cheek softly. "Good night."

This infernal paraffin lighting was just not enough for me. The rooms were only dimly lit and I still found myself fumbling around. I was suddenly distracted. I smelt smoke. I sniffed the lamp. I never found the lights that potent. I quickly opened the door and followed the permeating smell. I could see a billow of smoke ascending the far corridor stairs.

There was an antiquated alarm on the wall, a red handle in a small box. I pulled it with all my might but nothing happened. The smoke was getting thicker. Chad was soon running towards me. He had smelt the smoke too.

"Mary, get the boys out. I'll see what I can do with the fire. It seems small." He grabbed the fire extinguisher and I saw him disappear down the smokey flight of stairs.

"Please be careful, Chad."

"Always am, Mary."

I ran down the stairs near my rooms and ran along to the end rooms nearest the fire. I burst through the door: "Get up boys, fire alarm." I tried to remove any panic from my voice. It was the younger boys' dormitory and smoke was beginning to creep through their door. "Quickly boys now, quickly." I gathered them together and the senior boys next door had already sensed a commotion and were in the corridor.

"Get the boys downstairs and out of house." Immediately the senior boys grabbed a junior by the hand and quickly led them down the stairs. "Get right out of the house boys. Don't stop."

The corridor below had been evacuated by Mr Chapman and the bottom floor by Miss Simms. Some boys were coughing and gasping for air as they made their way downstairs. Most boys had bare feet and no dressing gowns. I started to worry as Chad had still not returned. One old fashioned fire extinguisher and a non working alarm would not be enough. As I moved towards the far end, flames had now appeared and suddenly caught hold of the curtains by the stairs. Part of the ceiling was now on fire. I yelled for Chad. I had no idea how long I could remain on this top corridor. I yelled again there was no response.

I turned to make my way down the stairs I heard faint coughing. A boy must have been left behind. I ran to my room grabbed a torch and made my way onto the smoke filled floor below. I knocked on each door. The smoke made it difficult to yell. I tried to cover my mouth and nose to try and defeat any inhalation. I got half way along the corridor when part of the ceiling collapsed in front of me. There was no way I would be able the find Chad or the missing boy. I ran back to the stairs I'd come from and ran two at a time out into the courtyard. I could hear the siren of the fire engine and ambulance service. Due to our location the fire services' response would always take longer.

Many of the boys seemed in shock while a few of the younger ones huddled together. Miss Simms was trying her best to comfort those in distress and deal with any physical injuries. This was the only time during my post here that I was impressed by her calm under fire and her dealings with highly distressed junior boys.

I looked around to see Chad. I could not see him anywhere. I had left him only five minutes ago but it seemed like forever. The Headmaster took roll call. Two junior boys were missing. They must have been on the corridor I evacuated. I felt sick; I felt dizzy, I should have found them when I heard them. Michael was also missing. I assumed that sleeping in sick bay; Miss Simms would have alerted him. I braced myself for the news of all four.

The fire brigade entered the building knowing that we had two children and one adult missing. There was a small explosion which blew out the upper windows furthest away. The fire had taken a firm hold of that area of the house. Minutes later Chad staggered through the front door with a young boy in his arms.

"Chad, oh my God! Are you alright?" It seemed pathetic to ask. He gently handed over the boy to the ambulance crew, and literally fell against me. He was coughing and spluttering but I held him for as long as I could. I looked down and saw that his shirt was burnt up to the elbow.

"I had to push the flames away from the boy." I just started crying unsure of what emotion I should be feeling at this time. "I only found one of the boys," he said in exasperation. "I heard him crying. I couldn't find him through the smoke."

"You did more than you should, Chad. You must have that burn seen to." I walked with him to the ambulance.

"Michael?" he asked.

"Not found yet, nor the other boy," I said sadly.

I looked to the house which the fire crew had now gotten under control, and just saw smoke billowing out of the missing windows. I turned back to Chad when a boy then shouted, "Moorcroft!" I turned to the front door and out walked Michael carrying the other boy. A fireman rushed up and scooped the boy from Michael's arms.

I left Chad in the ambulance and hastened to Michael who by now was kneeling on the floor. He was wheezing and trying to gulp the air. I knelt down beside him, encasing his now black face in my hands.

"Where have you been? Where did you find the boy?" I knew I was asking too many questions. One of the firemen came over to me.

"He is a very brave lad. He did a great job in there. You should be really proud of him."

"Thank you I am." I just stopped for a second. I was proud of him. Realisation hit, my whole body shook with pride.

"Let us get you seen to." I helped him off the floor.

"I'm fine thanks. I don't need to see anyone," he protested.

The Headmaster came over to us.

"Good lad," he quietly mustered. "Where did you find the boy? Well, well done." And then he moved off as quickly as he could.

"He was hiding in the bathroom on the top corridor. He was in the bathroom when everybody evacuated. I came up to see you. I heard him and we waited until we could find our way out. It was nothing."

"Why come up to see me?" I asked bewildered.

"I wanted to make sure you were alright," he said with such conviction that I just pulled him into my chest and hugged him tightly.

By now most of the boys were cold and tired. We were able to move everybody into the hall. The fire was completely out. The area cordoned off. Most of the top corridor, including my rooms, was ruined by soot damage. I had the clothes that I stood up in. The boys' dormitories furthest from the fire were unharmed. It would take weeks before we could move back.

The fire originated in the linen closet near the back fire escape. It was more a room than a closet. Boys were known to go in there to smoke. Chad and the two junior boys were taken to the local hospital. Chad was back that same night. The boys were kept overnight. I was told just to keep an eye on Michael. Well this transferred over to Miss Simms who was able to move back to the sickbay taking Michael with her.

It was around 3am when the boys finally got to sleep. I was to share with Miss Simms for the next few weeks. I would rather have stayed in a burnt out room than share with Miss Simms.

"I'm not happy with this arrangement either, Miss Kendall, but it was the Headmaster's decision."

"It is fine Miss Simms," I lied.

"Well if you could keep to your side of the room," she pointed to a small corner in her small room. "I go to bed at 10.30 so ensure you are quiet when you come back in."

"Yes, of course." It was easier to agree than lie.

"Moorcroft is next door. The key for the door is in the top drawer," she pointed to her dresser.

"You lock him in?" I said in disbelief.

"Of course. There is no way he is going to wander from me."

"That is illegal. You can't lock a boy in a room. How did he get out during the fire?"

"I let him out and surprise, surprise he wandered off."

I stared at her in disbelief. He's locked up like a caged animal. I would speak to the Headmaster in the morning. For the time being I just wanted to sleep.

CHAPTER TWELVE

Later that morning we sorted the boys out with clothes and sent them off to class and notified their parents. The Headmaster had left early for a meeting that morning so I had to wait until I could discuss Michael being locked in. Not only did I feel the stress from the fire but my mother's neighbour rang. My mother had fallen down the stairs and had broken her ankle. I was needed to run errands and sort out Edward which she was unable to do.

I hurried to the Headmaster's new secretary, a woman called Miss Cripps, who was at least fifty years old and very crabby. I made my excuse and made arrangements for my immediate departure. Chad had the next two periods free and offered to drive me to the station.

"I can drive you all the way if you wish."

"No thanks, Chad, I will be fine. You'll keep an eye on Michael won't you?" I stared right in his face when I spoke.

"Yes. He certainly redeemed himself last night. He is a brave lad. I wouldn't let anything happen to him, okay?"

I nodded in the knowledge he would. I just caught the train and was at home by the early afternoon. Edward was quite unsettled as a nurse had been in to tend to Mum. Strangers upset him terribly. Mum did what she could but was unable to walk unassisted. Edward came straight to me as soon as I was in the front door. I signed to him that everything was alright now and I was here for the next few days. He wandered off to paint and I settled myself in. I told Mum about the fire. While home it also gave me a chance to buy some new clothes.

The following day I went into York, primarily for clothes to replace those damaged. I took my time and pondered on my relationship with Chad and with Michael. I stopped at a cafe and saw some university students on their laptops and very jazzy phones. I wondered: would I be able to find out the circumstances of Michael's mother's death? I had only been given snippets of information. I decided to do a little investigation of my own. I had no access to a computer apart from going to the local library.

I found myself a computer in the library to use and typed in his mother's name and the word 'murdered' and saw what materialised from that. Several entries came up so I systematically went through them. I must have been there nigh on two hours when I finally had a substantial hit from one of the London papers. It read:

15 July 1998

MURDER OF PROMINET QC IN BAYSWATER

A murder enquiry has been launched after a prominent QC was found strangled in the basement of her own house in Bayswater, London. The body of Penelope Moorcroft, 46, a barrister at Loxely Chambers, Lincolns Inn Fields was found by her husband. She lived with her husband, Anton, and their adopted son, Michael, aged 9. There were no signs of forced entry into the house. The police believe the suspect to be some-one that she knew. Her body was found naked. There is no indication of her being sexually assaulted. Their son Michael was found by her husband lying over his dead mother's body. He is now in the care of a grandparent.

At present according to police there are no leads although her husband is helping the police with their inquiries. A possible suspect was spotted leaving the premises at around 3.30pm. He is believed to be in middle to late forties, around 6ft tall, slim build, grey-ing hair and a sporting a small moustache. He was wearing a white shirt, black trousers and carried a tan briefcase. The police urge this man to make himself known to the police so that he can be eliminated from their enquiries.

Penelope Moorcroft was trying a very complex case at the time of her death. It is feared that retribution may be a contributing factor. Police are working closely with the courts pertaining to that specific case. Anton Moorcroft, 47, a partner of PriceWaterhouseCoopers,

London was considered by neighbours to be a worka-
holic not returning from work until late evening, sometimes the early morning. Penelope Moorcroft was
according to neighbours a very sociable woman and
often had male visitors in her home during the day.
They adopted their son, Michael, two years ago after
the tragic death of his parents.

Any information regarding this murder should be
passed onto the police.

One thing leapt from the page. Michael was adopted.
No-one at school had mentioned this. It seemed that the
situation with him would forever be difficult. I tried
to find out at what age he was adopted. There was no
information available. I would only have to ask him.
I continued to search for any other information about
the murder. I was just about to call it a day when I came
upon another small article, it read:

27th August 1998

NO SUSPECTS IN QC'S MURDER BUT
FRAUDULENT ACTIVITY SUSPECTED

Police are still searching for the suspect of the murder
of Penelope Moorcroft QC, a prominent barrister, in
Bayswater last month. The police have followed a
couple of leads but nothing substantial has arisen.
Clients of Mrs Moorcroft have also been questioned.
Neighbours of the Moorcrofts' remarked that they were
a very sociable couple. Details of visitors have not been
made available at this time.

Mr Anton Moorcroft, a Senior Partner with PriceWaterhouseCoopers was discounted from their enquiries
as the main suspect. He was however found in posses-
sion of documents pertaining to a fraudulent account
at PriceWaterhouseCoopers showing a deficit in the
region of two million pounds. It is reported that he was
siphoning off money from the firm's Pension Fund and
Expense Account. If convicted he could receive a
sentence of up to ten years in prison. The Moorcrofts'
six bedroom home, their holiday home in Scotland and
two vintage Aston Martins will be used as assets if
found guilty of the charges.

The Moorcrofts' adopted son, Michael, was handed
over to social services shortly after his grandmother
died last month of natural causes. He will remain with
them until at least his father's court date. People fear
that the tragic past of this boy will continue into the
future.

The library needed to close I had been there almost four
hours. I was determined now to find out where his father
was presently and whether his mother's murderer had
been found. The librarian threw me an annoyed glance.
I just had ten more minutes to find out. I had trawled
through the court cases at the time and found nothing
but luckily found a small inclusion in the London paper
I had been already been reading. It clarified everything.
His father was arrested for fraud and was released on
bail of £100,000. Michael was still in the hands of social
services and in and out of foster homes in London. Two
years later, after a highly complex trial, his father was
found guilty of fraud and sentenced to eight years in

Welham Open Prison. Their house and sports cars were handed over to the Courts. His father was eventually released on parole three and a half years later. His current whereabouts were unknown. This family had lost extreme success and prosperity.

I had no idea that he was the Moorcrofts' adopted son. By now I was completely hooked. Where had Michael come from? Who gave birth to him? I heard a small bell ring near the door; it was time to go. I was supposed to be travelling back to school tomorrow evening. I would spend the day tomorrow wading through the newspapers for anything at all. I would ask Chad to come and drive me back to school. I had so much to tell him.

I arrived back at home and my mother was trying to chase Edward while stuck in the foot cast. Edward sometimes had a problem with bathing. He just wouldn't do it. We used to let him smell for a while but soon the stench would get to us. My mother would usually win with him but on one foot it was hopeless. I signed to Edward that he had a have a bath now and I was going to do it. He kept signing no at me. I ran the bath, shut the door to prevent his escape and in next to no time he was in the bath, cleaned and in bed. The process usually only took about 10 minutes, but due to my mother's absence it was nigh on 40 minutes. He was in bed by eight o'clock.

I used to tell my mother everything. We had and still have a close relationship but I could not tell her about Michael. I mentioned Chad and her whole face lit up. She had married me off in minutes. I phoned Chad. He was able to pick me. He sensed the excitement in my voice. The rebuild of the far side of the house was well on its way. The fire had been caused by a lit cigarette. Of course everyone jumped to blame Michael. Miss Simms had had him locked in sickbay. He could not possibly be in two places at once. I went to be with a satisfied grin on my face after my day investigating.

The next morning I was up early and back down to the library. It was the same severe woman on the reception desk as I pulled in my chair and set to work. The easiest thing to do was Google Michael's name and see if anything came up. There were about 30,000 hits on his name so I started to add his mother's name and place of work. No joy. I added his father. Nothing surfaced. I was getting more irritable and disappointed when I added Bramleigh School to the search. There were five hits but only one relevant to me. There was a picture of a small boy standing beside a grand piano jubilant holding a rather large trophy. Underneath the picture read:

PIANO PROTEGE MADE ORPHAN

This is the jubilant picture of piano protégé Michael Pattinson after the win of the Grand Prize at the Championship Music Festival in Glasgow. Michael is only seven years old. Michael travelled with a group of gifted children from London by coach. Tragedy struck when Michael's parents Lydia and Jeremy Pattinson were on their way to see their son perform. They were then going to continue on to a holiday in the Highlands. The couple never made it to their son's recital. A high sided lorry travelling along the M6 swerved in front of the

Pattinsons' car. They were unable to stop the impact. Both the lorry driver and Jeremy Pattinson were pronounced dead at the scene. Lydia Pattinson was taken by air ambulance to Glasgow Royal Infirmary with extensive injures but died later in intensive care. Michael was placed with his maternal grandmother, 72, but will be put up for adoption due to his grandmother's ill health. It is believed that no other family members could be traced. The lorry driver, Marcus Brodie, 45 leaves behind a two year old son and six month old baby girl. Investigators are still unsure as to why Mr Brodie swerved across the carriage way. The two lanes were closed for around six hours causing tale backs of several miles.

I wiped a tear from my eye. This boy would not want to get close to anyone. He had had so many losses. The loss of someone else must surely make him fear those who want to get close to him. I, like most people, argue and sometimes hate their family but I cannot imagine a world without the rest of mine.

Chad picked me up from my mother's at 7pm. He was eager to meet Edward and my mother. My mother greeted him warmly, carefully sizing him up as a potential future husband for me. Chad was very gracious. Edward initially was upset, rocking himself on the spot when he first walked through the door. Chad did not move towards him. I signed that he was my friend and left it at that. I pulled Chad into the kitchen to tell him of my trips to the library and what I had unearthed.

"What has got you so excited?" he said as he sat down at the kitchen table.

"I went to the library this morning. I should have been shopping for clothes but I looked up the murder of Michael's mother on the Internet and....."

"Welcome to technology at last Mary, it was going to happen sometime." I shushed him and carried on with my story.

"I know, just listen will you. Did you know his mother was a QC in London?"

"A what!"

"Barrister; very high up in the food chain; attorney to you Americans."

"Oh right. So?"

"Well his father, during investigations was found guilty of embezzling two million pounds. He was sent to prison for eight years. Michael went to a prep school in Kensington. We are talking wealthy plus. Why was he sent to us here? He was probably destined for Eton or Harrow."

"I still don't get you, Mary." I sat directly opposite, handing him a cup of tea.

"Michael was their adopted son."

"You are kidding me?" he looked at me in disbelief.

"That is not all. Michael is a child protégé; extreme intelligence; sky high IQ and a pianist of my ex fiancée's level.

His birth parents died in a car crash on the way to a music competition in Glasgow."

"I still don't know what you are saying." He looked at me confused.

"Honestly, Chad, I worry about you sometimes. He must be bored rigid at our second rate public school. Boredom can be very destructive. He is holed up in school, unable to go out or mix with any youngster of his intelligence. Don't you see he has nothing and no one to challenge him?"

"So you are saying he's badly behaved and more than a little strange, I might add, because he is more intelligent than everyone else, staff included?"

"It makes perfect sense to me. He was sent to us because his father went to prison and he lost everything. This was all he could afford. He is intelligent enough for the top public schools with monetary help. A scholarship would be so easy for him."

"Look, Mary. I think you are reading far too much into this. Sure the kids had a hard life so far but he is far from being normal; there is something very creepy about the way he stares at you. That's all I'm saying."

"I thought you could help. You're the maths genius; challenge his capabilities."

"I don't know anything about gifted kids, Mary. I wouldn't know what to do with him." He folded his arms in which could only have been frustration.

"Please try, Chad. Just for me?"

"He lives in a completely different universe from normal people, Mary. You know they are blaming him for the fire the other evening. Look it is his final year. He has only months to go before he leaves for good. Then he will be someone else's problem."

"Miss Simms had him locked in sickbay, Chad," I shouted at him.

He looked sheepish, "I know, Mary, we all do apart from you. It was agreed upon when you were not there."

"What?" I was exasperated, "Why was I not asked?"

"Because we all knew what your reaction would be. It's best for him and for the school. At least we know where he is at night."

"That does not justify him being locked up." By now I was incensed, "What about the fire risk?"

"Margaret got him out."

"Oh that's okay is it?"

"Mary, please relax; don't act like this. No one is against you. The Head knows that you are very fond of him and didn't want you to have to make a decision. Be reasonable."

"Reasonable is locking a child in a room is it? I'm not surprised he hates you all. This is so wrong and having that vile harpie look after him. She's an evil woman, Chad."

"She's been called a lot worse than that."

"I don't know how you can so flippant about all this?" My legs were beginning to shake under the table with such anger.

"I'm sorry, Mary, but I can't help the way I feel about him. All that you have told me doesn't endear him to me any more than before. You care too much, Mary."

"And you not at all."

"Don't say that. Look let's get back to school otherwise that witch will probably cast a spell on you." As always Chad was able to draw a smile out of me when I really didn't want to.

The car drive back was quiet with a little discomfort thrown in. As things go with Chad this was short lived and he was back to his usual self. We arrived back at school in plenty of time. Miss Simms was still putting the younger boys to bed so I ran myself a hot bubble bath and poured myself a sneaky glass of wine. I couldn't relax. My mind was still reeling from what I had read and the conversation I'd had with Chad. I was in bed by 9.30. I could still hear the senior boys on the floor above.

Once Miss Simms was back, I pretended to be asleep. She waddled about for at least half an hour before she eventually got into bed. I could not sleep. Miss Simms' snoring didn't help. I laid awake for what seemed like an eternity before I made the decision to get up and out of the building. I was careful not to wake Miss Simms, although the noise she made could probably wake the whole school. I threw my dressing gown and slippers on and grabbed paraffin light. As I reached the door handle Miss Simms suddenly rolled over onto her side taking an enormous breath. It was like watching a beached whale.

Once out the door I had no idea where to go. I opted for the private garden outside the staff common room. I wouldn't be seen there and it would certainly be quiet in order to let me think. I made it down to the staffroom without being noticed and quickly went out the small door behind the curtains. I sat down on one of the wooden benches. I wished I had bought a blanket as it was really quite cold but refreshing nevertheless. Suddenly I heard a rustling noise.

"Hello Mary."

I turned to look: it was Michael. He was fully dressed in school uniform.

"You scared me Michael. What are you doing out here?"

"I can say the same for you?" he smirked.

"How did you get out here? Wait a minute how did you get out of sick bay?"

He opened his palm. There was a large bunch of keys.

"I have my own set of keys. I bought them off a senior boy in my first year. They've been so good to me," he smiled caressing them. "I often go out at night; you?"

"Not so often." I shook my head slightly.

"It's good to mull over things. Think about our place in the world."

"And where is your place, Michael?"

"Ah that is my secret. Do you feel cold?"

My whole body was beginning to shake and my teeth chatter. "No I'm fine," I lied.

He took off his blazer and wrapped it around my shoulders. He sat down next to me, our bodies touching.

"Why are you in uniform?"

"Well I had to put something on besides I never changed for bed anyway. The wicked witch locked me in sickbay after prep and I was out of this place five minutes later. She never checks on me."

"Where do you go, Michael?"

"Out and about." He was stalling.

"Miss Simms has found you sitting in the library. I can't believe it is the books that lead you there."

He shrugged, "No you're quite right, it's not the books. Someone I loved very much loved to read. It reminds me of her. I can feel close to her."

It was now or never, "Your real mother?"

He immediately stood up. "How do you know about that?" He did not seem angry just surprised.

"I'm so sorry, Michael, I found out by default. I don't mean to upset you."

He sat back down next to me: "She was an extraordinarily kind and selfless woman. I miss her; and him."

I put my arm around his shoulders and he rested his head against me. I could feel the beating of his heart and the gentleness of his breathing. I wanted to stay like this forever.

"What about your adoptive parents?"

"Let's just say they were different."

"Where will you go after you leave here? You will be eighteen and no more foster parents. It is not too late to apply for university. Or do you want to get a job and miss the great overrated university experience. I can see you as a teacher."

"No thanks," he laughed. "I do have plans though. Ones I can't share with you now. Suffice to say I'm a free spirit, I'll go where life takes me."

"What about your adoptive father? Does he keep in contact with you?"

"During his first year in prison he used to write to me. I visited him once. I don't care for him much. His job was far more important than me. Anyone can adopt a child nowadays."

I sensed the sadness in his voice.

"Mary?"

"Yes, Michael."

"Your brother; how does that work? I mean how do you live with someone who cannot communicate with you?"

"Oh he can communicate. I sign, so does my mother. He lives in his own world, a world that we are not part off. He still has a personality and qualities that any human has. He's my twin, and I cannot imagine what it would be like if something happened to him. We just have patience with him. He gets a lot of love in our family. We would be incomplete without him. He is also deaf which can confuse things sometimes but we manage."

"I thought they put people like him in hospital."

"Autistic people can live a life with family. Some live in a group supervised home, it is not always the best place but they have experienced carers."

"But your brother?"

"He will live with us until my mother passes or he miraculously becomes better."

I could feel my eyes welling up and so I quickly changed the subject.

"How did you end up with the bunch of misfits you go around with?"

"How does anyone become friends? In the first year you cling onto anyone and as the years pass you dump the ones who don't live up to your expectations. That didn't happen for us. We met on the first day. We all managed to get detention in the first week and that was it. Friends until the end."

It was getting late. I lifted his head off my shoulder.

"Come on. Let's get back to our own prison." I smiled broadly at him, "It's getting late."

We walked back inside; I locked the door behind me. We quietly wandered back to sickbay and snuck in. Miss Simms was sleeping soundly.

"Goodnight, Michael."

"Goodnight, Mary." He opened the adjoining door and closed it quietly behind me.

I was asleep within minutes.

CHAPTER THIRTEEN

I saw Michael in class later that morning. He seemed fine, unlike the visible tiredness in me. During class we would share a moment as his smile lit up mine. Our relationship so far had gone undetected. Chad knew of sorts but not everything.

There was a staff meeting at break. The end of term was only weeks away. The boys would sit their final exams next week. It was also time for staff to nominate outstanding pupils who would join the alumni on the walls. I wanted to nominate Michael as the top of English literature. I knew however that this would not be mutually agreed. The Headmaster arrived and the sports prize needed to be awarded.

"So do we have a name for sports?" he looked up from his file.

"I would like to nominate Michael Moorcroft," I couldn't have heard correctly. Chad was just behind me, "He is an asset to the cricket team. He always turns up and the other boys seem to admire him." I looked over my shoulder. Chad was beaming a bright smile at me. I mouthed him a thank you.

"Well, does anybody have a problem with him as the winner of the sports prize?" He looked around him, expecting a deluge of negative comments. None were forth coming.

"Well that is settled then. While we are talking about Moorcroft, at the end of term social services will transfer him to adult services. They will take up from child services. They will find him suitable accommodation. Has he got a place at university, Mary?"

"He did not apply Headmaster, but does say he has plans. What they are I don't know."

"Okay, just keep me posted. I, for one, cannot wait until this boy is out of this school."

There were general nods of agreement. I felt Chad's hand on my shoulder and a light squeeze.

The meeting ended and Chad and I went out into the garden.

"I want to do more for him, Chad."

"You have done more than enough. You've been the mother to that boy. He's leaving school. You have to let him go."

"I know but it is so hard, Chad. I love him."

"That is your problem. Come let's get inside and teach something!" he laughed. He laughed and I was dying inside.

That night I had gone to bed late after grading papers. Miss Simms was fast asleep. I heard a small knock at the door. I stood up from the desk and opened the door.

"Chad! What are you doing here?"

"Have you checked sleeping beauty tonight?"

"Yes, earlier."

"Well he is gone. Two junior boys saw him leave about half an hour ago. They came to tell me. Get your coat. We will try and get him back before anyone else knows he's gone. Grab a couple of the paraffin lights."

"Okay, I know where he goes." I pulled on my jacket and shoes. "I'm ready now."

It's impossible to see a lot on the moors and one lot of rocks looks awfully like another.

"He has gone to the Clearwater Lake. It is about a mile from the school."

We found ourselves stumbling over mosses, rocks and piles of, God knows what.

"I cannot see a bloody thing, Mary. How are we going to spot him?" he moaned.

"We will see him, Chad."

"You are going to owe me big time, Mary. What if he is not there? Are we going to stumble around until it is daylight?"

"You are such a wimp, Chad. You're not afraid of the dark are you?"

"Well as a matter of fact it has been a childhood phobia of mine," he laughed. I didn't know whether he was serious.

I stopped suddenly. "Please tell me that we are not lost," said Chad.

"It should be here. Let's turn about and retrace our steps. He could be hurt or lying in a bog somewhere."

"That is highly unlikely if he has been going here for years. It's us that are panicking not him."

We retraced our steps and I recognized a large rock formation. Everything looked exactly the same.

"We should have turned left here rather than straight ahead."

"How on earth do you know that? Oh great; now it's raining!" It began to spit with rain.

"Call it feminine intuition."

"Believe me, Mary; I'm never going to listen to a woman giving directions again."

"Shh, I think I hear some water. Down here." I pointed the way, "This could be it Chad."

"I bloody well hope so," he was getting increasing bad tempered.

"Careful, we must not frighten him."

"I don't believe he is the frightened sort."

We carried on walking and there in the moonlight was Michael, stripped naked, his back to us with his palms up. I noticed his clothes lying beside the edge of the water. The skies were clear and there were a few stars. Staring at stars always made me feel small and insignificant but this was no time for star gazing. Chad whispered to me that something was resting on Michael's right palm. We could not make out what it was. Although our lights were fairly bright, he seemed undisturbed. He remained motionless, his head up pointing to those stars.

"Michael," I called softly. He did not respond I tried again: "Michael, its Mary."

We advanced towards the edge of the water. He slowly turned his head towards us and then returned to his original position. His skin was white as milk. There was a faint sound of the water lapping around his waist.

"Michael, please look at us."

"Mary," said Chad panicked, "the object in his hand is a knife."

"Oh God, Chad get him out of there."

"What do you suggest?" he replied sarcastically.

"Get in there Chad. Stop him!"

I looked at Michael. He lifted the hand with the knife up to his chest. It all happened so quickly. I did not feel Chad leave my side. All I saw was Chad diving on Michael. Water exploded everywhere. I was soaked to the skin. Chad pulled Michael out of the water and both sat on the wet moss. Chad was breathing heavily and Michael sat spluttering out the water which he had swallowed.

Chad looked at me, "Come on Mary, you didn't think I would not try and help you did you?"

I was so relieved that both were fine. I left Chad sorting himself out and sat down beside Michael. The rain was now pouring. It didn't seem to bother him in the least.

"Michael, are you okay?" I took my jacket off and put it around his shoulders. He looked down at the ground and began to pick at the moss in front of him. "Please answer me." He was in a trance like state.

"Chad, do you think he can hear us?"

"I don't know," he sighed. "Perhaps he is sleepwalking?"

"What? We are a mile away from school, Chad; he would be in the dark with no light."

"I'm just trying to help."

"I know I'm sorry, let's get back to school."

Chad picked up Michael from the floor and stood him on his feet. Michael suddenly looked at me his eyes wide open. "What are you doing here, Miss?"

"We were looking for you. What are you doing here?" I asked him firmly.

"This is my church." He waved his arm indicating the enclosed landscape around the water.

Chad rolled his eyes. So much for the sleepwalking theory. Chad whispered in my ear, "He is crazy, Mary."

The rain was pelting it down by now. It began to thunder. There we stood on the Yorkshire Moors with Chad soaked to the skin and me shaking with the cold and a wet and deluded adolescent. We managed to find our weary way back to the school. Never had it looked so inviting.

"Doesn't it remind you, Mary, of our first meeting?" smiled Chad.

"How could I forget," I laughed.

On our return we went up to Chad's room to warm up. I was expecting to see an American college boy's room but I was pleasantly surprised. It was full to the ceiling with books. There were two leather armchairs placed in front of the fire. I pushed Michael into the room. Chad grabbed some towels from his bathroom for Michael.

"Excuse me, I'll just get changed. You can use this dressing gown for him." He threw it at us and went into his bedroom and shut the door.

"Let's get those wet things off." Unlike the last time, he took off my jacket and rubbed himself down with the towel. He put on the dressing gown and perched himself on the edge of one of the armchairs. I grabbed one of Chad's shirts and made for the bathroom to change. Michael's eyes never left me. When both Chad and I were back in the room we looked at each other. Chad poured both of us a medicinal whiskey to help in our decision making.

"What shall we do with him now?" he asked exasperated.

"We leave him to warm up and I will take him back to sickbay."

"And were going to say nothing?"

"Yes, it is graduation in two days' time. The Head knows my feeling about the whole thing."

"The Head told me that after graduation he will be handed over to adult social services and he will be their responsibility. The Head has noted your feelings down. There is a huge file, Mary. I'm pretty sure social services will see that the kid is extremely strange."

"Chad, he is in the room!" I barked at him.

"Even so, let us just get to graduation okay?"

"Okay. Come, Michael, we need to be back in our rooms now."

I gave the empty glass back to Chad. It did make me feel marginally better.

"Thanks again Chad, for what you did."

"No sweat, you better get going."

I grabbed Michael's hand and made our way the sickbay. I ensured he was in bed and settled then crept into mine with great relief.

Chapter Fourteen

The week before graduation was always very busy. Reports to parents had to be finished and the end of term exams for the younger boys marked. Michael's year had finished all their work so were free to roam; except Michael, of course. He was confined to the library where he would also be seen all day by the librarian, Mr Carrington. I snuck in most afternoons and kept him company.

"Mary?" yelled Chad during our library session.

"Shh," uttered Mr Carrington.

"Sorry, Mary." He sat down with both of us. "How about you and I go the little restaurant this Friday night? I need to be back for 9pm but it would give us a couple of hours at least. What do you say?"

"That sounds great Chad," I said a little too loudly.

"Shhh."

"Sorry!" we both said at the same time. Michael sat there silent but a wry smile across his face.

I was able to get back into my rooms on the top corridor on the Thursday. Thankfully although there was some soot damage but generally the room was fine. I looked in my wardrobe for something to wear to dinner. A lot of things I had had to throw away but these were non essentials and completely replaceable. I spent the afternoon with Michael as I had two free periods. I was able to look busy as I had my reports to write. Michael sat with me reading a mammoth book. I occasionally took his hand and held it under the table.

"Michael, are you worried about what will happen when you leave here?" I whispered.

"Don't worry about me, Mary. I have it all figured out," he said with great conviction.

I was finally able to sleep in my room. Without the fanfare of noise from Miss Simms I was able to sleep much more soundly. On Friday the boys' trunks would be packed in preparation for Saturday. The parents would arrive in the morning in time for the prize giving and to take their boys home for the summer. I was busy helping some of the junior boys pack their dirty clothes into their trunks.

At 6pm Chad pulled his car up at the entrance and we took off for the restaurant in Hawksmoore. It is so much nicer travelling in an open top car on a glorious evening. We were given the same table as last time. We had just ordered drinks when Chad took my hand.

"Mary, there is something I need to tell you." He face looked serious.

"Okay. What is it?"

"I've really enjoyed the year with you. You are such a ray of sunshine in an otherwise dark and dreary place. It was like living in a Dickens' novel. A woman who is so much a woman has been sorely missed around here. The thing is that I have been offered a college teaching post for next term."

"That sounds great. Where is the college? York?"

"I'm afraid not. It's in Chicago. I'm going to America." My face dropped.

"The thing is, Mary, I haven't decided whether to take it or not. I cannot stay here and just be your friend. I love you Mary. Can you see it in your heart to eventually love me?"

I took his face in my hands, "Chad I love you as a friend; a truly great friend. You make me laugh and I could not have stayed here to teach if it was not for you. I'm so sorry Chad."

"Well I thought it was important to ask you. I'm sorry if I have embarrassed you..."

"I'm not embarrassed, I'm flattered but I'm not embarrassed." I looked into his eyes, "You are a gifted beautiful man and those girls in Chicago are just going to love you."

He stifled a small laugh and tried to wipe what I thought was a tear away from his eye.

"Thanks, Mary."

"Well let's get ordering I'm starving." I smiled the biggest smile I could and he forced a small smile back.

We left the restaurant around 8pm so Chad would be in time to put the seniors to bed. The drive back was quiet and surprisingly not uncomfortable. I would miss Chad terribly and I couldn't image life at Bramleigh without him. As we came up the drive we could see flashing lights.

"I wonder what's going on. Perhaps one of the boys has been injured or taken ill," I said to Chad.

We entered the courtyard and Chad pulled the car into an alcove to be out the way of an ambulance. As we entered the school hall it was pandemonium. The Headmaster's secretary, Mrs Cripps, was wringing her hands and pacing up and down.

"What is it Sylvia? What's happened?"

"It is that Moorcrom, Moorwood boy?"

"You mean Moorcroft?" I asked getting panicky.

"He stabbed the Head."

"What!" I said in disbelief.

"The ambulance crew are with him, there is blood everywhere. It doesn't look good."

I grabbed Chad's arm and pulled him into the Headmaster's office. The Headmaster lay on the floor, covered in blood. The ambulance crew were busying to stop the blood. What was more shocking was Michael sitting on the floor, rocking himself quickly back and forth holding a bloody knife in his palm. I could hear the police siren as it approached the school.

I leant down on one knee and tried to ply the knife out of his hand.

"Let go of the knife, Michael!"

There was no response, "Michael, sweetheart let go of the knife." I took his hand and he lightly dropped it into my hand, "Good boy."

By now two police officers had arrived. A female constable came over to assist me with Michael. He did not stop rocking. I put my whole weight behind him and gradually bought him to a stop. His eyes were staring blankly ahead lifeless.

The second constable crouched over the paramedics to ascertain their position. It was felt that the Headmaster could now be removed to hospital as they had managed to stabilise his condition. They moved him out of the office. The police constables were now completely focused on Michael. He had not moved from the floor. He now had the hint of a smile on his face. I put it down to shock.

"What is the young gentleman's name?" asked the female officer.

"Michael James Moorcroft," I replied.

"How old is he?"

"Just turned 18."

"Did anybody witness this incident?"

"Mrs Cripps was just outside when Michael was in the Headmaster's office. I think she heard the commotion."

The officer pointed to the knife I held, "Is this the weapon?"

"Yes, he was holding it in his hand when we came in."

"Any reason why he did this?" He was staring at Michael, hoping for some answer.

"We have no idea. I know they don't particularly get on but that is most pupil and teacher relationships, isn't?"

"Does he have a mental illness or disability?"

"He has been very strange officer all year," interjected Chad.

The two officers could only stare at this very strange boy. He had uttered not one word since we had entered the room.

"What will happen now, Officer?" I asked concerned.

"He will be arrested and taken to the police station to be charged. A police doctor will examine him and a decision will then be taken as to where he will reside before a court appearance."

I was not able to talk to Michael alone before the police escorted him to the station in town. He sat and started rocking back and forth again. His eyes fixed on me with an inappropriate smile on his face. I truly believed that he was not aware of his actions or the seriousness of what he had done. I sat beside him and took his hand in mine.

"Michael, do you know what is happening?" No response. "They are going to take you to the police station and you will be asked some important questions."

It was useless trying to talk with him; I was met with stoney silence each time. One of the officers hoisted him off the floor. He was handcuffed and read his rights. I don't believe he even heard them. Michael did not resist. He did exactly as he was told but fixed his gaze on me. It seemed that there was nothing of him left.

I was alarmed about the force of the officer placing the handcuffs. "Officer is that really necessary? He's only a boy. I doubt he is going to run off anywhere."

"Sorry, Ma'am; just following procedure."

I tried questioning Michael again: "Can you tell me why you assaulted the Headmaster?" Again no response. He sat perched on a chair for a few minutes in silence. He suddenly rose from his chair and looked out of the window where he could see the waiting police car.

"We have to take him down to the station now to charge him. It will most likely be assault with a dangerous weapon or if the victim dies possibly manslaughter." They took the knife from me and bagged it as evidence. It was covered in blood.

"Is it going to be taken into account of his behavioural problems? That he is ill. He needs a hospital not a police cell. He barely understands what is going on."

"Miss, a police psychiatrist will see him at the station. If you wish to accompany him, that is fine. But he was caught sitting by the victim on this very floor holding a bloodied knife. The outlook doesn't look great does it?"

"He is ill officer and I will ensure this is vehemently voiced," I protested.

I looked at Chad; his concerned face somehow comforted me. "I will organise another member of staff to take over my shift and I will follow you down in fifteen minutes."

"Will you be alright, Mary?" He pulled me close to him and gave me a hug. My whole body was fraught with tension.

"Yes, Chad, I need to go. I must go. He needs me more than you do here. I'm staying right with him."

"Sorry, Ma'am," interrupted the officer, "we must go now."

"Yes of course. May I just get a jacket?" Chad automatically removed his jacket and placed it around my shoulders. I smiled weakly at him. "I will let you know."

"I'll be there, Mary. I won't leave you."

Sixty pairs of eyes stared at us from all available windows in the school. I tried to shield Michael as much as I could as I helped him into the back of the police car. I was determined to ensure that Michael would be seen as a young boy who had had exceptional circumstances growing up and that he now displayed behaviour not within his control. I turned to look at him. His eyes were dead ahead and fiercely focused on the policeman in front of him; on his lap his blood stained hands rested in a prayer position.

Upon arrival at the station he was booked in. I was led to a small interview room and brought a cup of milky tea in a plastic cup. Half an hour later I was given another. Brilliant; tea again! I doubt my problems and anxieties would dissipate with a cup of Typhoo. I must have been left staring at those four walls for more than an hour at least. Thankfully a tall, distinguished looking gentleman entered the room.

"Miss Kendall?"

"Yes."

"I'm Dr Collins. I work as a forensic psychiatrist. I understand you are responsible for this boy."

"Yes. He is incredibly troubled and somewhat damaged. He's had a rough time. Since I have worked at the school he has shown some very peculiar and disturbing behaviour."

"I'm afraid, Miss Kendall, that I have just been told that Mr Hanrahan has died. We are looking at a manslaughter charge. Obviously this is incredibly serious and I need to have as clear a picture as possible. You do realise at eighteen he will be tried in court as an adult? Please tell me as much as you can."

Words could not describe what I was feeling. A manslaughter charge. Prison. I just could not believe this was happening. I tried to tell him as much as I could.

"He disappears for days on end and can be found wandering the streets of the village. He has wandered onto the moors half dressed. He can be very uninhibited. He has been aggressive to pupils and students alike. He goes to the local lake to bathe and rid himself of his sins. Those are his words. He can sit and stare at nothing for hours on end. His upper body is covered in scars; believed to be self inflicted. He remains alone most of the time."

"I have seen the scars and indeed witnessed the incredible staring. What he seems to be exhibiting is a period of acute psychosis. It is a very serious illness and I will do all that I can for him. Has he seen any doctor recently? Anybody we need to liaise with?"

"No nothing has been done since I've been at the school."

"What about his parents?"

"His father was in prison, whereabouts unknown and his mother was murdered in their house."

"I recognise the name."

"She was a QC in London. Penelope Moorcroft."

"Yes of course, dreadful and they never found the perpetrator either. Very sad indeed."

"I believe that he is ill doctor. He would not have harmed the Head if he was well. I know him and he doesn't deserve prison. His life has been a terribly sad mess.

"I have spoken, and I use the term loosely, to Michael. He has not responded to my questioning and just sat staring at me. I will be taking the boy to Millhill psychiatric hospital for assessment. I need to know whether he is fit to plea in court. Following this, he will either be returned to the police for court proceedings or will remain with us at the hospital for an indeterminate period of time. From my brief time with him I would recommend that he stay with us; for a while at least. That is only my initial assessment but these things often take time to understand clearly. He will have a thorough assessment at the hospital. Often it is very difficult to make evaluations in custody as stress levels of the vulnerable begin to soar."

"Thank you doctor. May I see him?"

"I don't see why not. A short meeting would not hurt. I'll see you in a few minutes, Miss Kendall."

Chapter Fifteen

He left the room and I was full of hope that now this boy's future would be a lot more positive. I smiled a broad smile. He would become a patient rather than an inmate.

Moments later, Michael walked in.

"We're just outside the door if you need us," said the police constable who had escorted Michael in.

"Thank you, Officer."

It was a couple of minutes before he spoke.

"Bravo, Mary; bravo." I smiled sweetly at him. He was trying to clap with his handcuffs on. A wry smile crossed his face. I was momentarily stunned. "You are just so perfect." I was perplexed.

He continued, "I enjoyed doing it you know. It was such a rush." He did not seem to be under any stress or fear at all.

"Doing what?"

"Strangulation, stabbing, you choose." He sat down opposite me, placing his bloodstained hands on the desk.

"That poor excuse for a man. Stabbing is so much more messy. I can see now where I made the mistake. You know it is fascinating when you see the lips turning blue in strangulation. Well not so much blue as a purple colour. Wouldn't you agree with me, Mary?"

I couldn't breathe. I did not hear correctly. This was not the boy I knew sitting opposite me. I wanted to leave but was compelled to stay.

"Mary? The colour blue or a purple blue? It is quite simple." He honestly wanted an answer. An answer I could not give. "Well he deserved it the smarmy bastard. It is so frustrating that I didn't get the chance to finish him off. That bloody secretary of his interrupting all the time. Do you think anyone would miss him if he died? Well, he is just going to have to wait a little longer until our next meeting. Is he going to make it?"

"Michael, he's dead."

"Pity!"

"That's an awful thing to say."

"My apologies," he said sarcastically

My mouth dry, I could not function to reply, but I managed to utter the need for a solicitor.

"What fun would there be in that!" he laughed.

I pulled myself together as much as I was able. Thinking straight was not happening. He was relishing every moment of my horror and awkwardness.

"Why the Headmaster, Michael?"

"Oh come, come Mary. I thought you were intelligent. He was the bastard with my mother in the basement. I saw him clearly as he ran past me on the stairs. He was so fast leaving that he left his jacket and his wallet. The opportunity just could not be missed even if it was a little late in coming"

"Did he strangle your mother?" I asked in disbelief.

"I strangled my mother, Mary," he said with jubilation. "He was not the first of my mother's conquests. My mother was a whore. The timing was perfect. Her naked body; just lying there with him. It repulsed me. She was a slut, like most women wouldn't you agree? Don't pretend I do not know what is happening between you and Chad. It's all over school you know. Tell me all about it." He clasped his hands together on the desk and gently rested his chin on them, "So, Mary, what are you? Lovers? Friends? Will there be a wedding? I do hope so." He smiled knowingly like a cheeky schoolboy. "Do tell; I feel like I know you both so well. The way you look at each other." He was enjoying every moment of my distress.

"Stop it."

"Come. Come now don't be shy."

"You're not going to get away with this."

"You helped it happen. After seven years my dream finally came true." He moved closer to me and gently

135

pushed a strand of hair away from my face. "Are you afraid of me, Mary?"

I whispered a small yes. He was so close I could smell the dried blood on his hands.

"Michael. You couldn't kill your mother. You were 11 years old, how could you strangle a grown woman, surely she would have overpowered you?" He had to be making this up. Under stress he was admitting to something he didn't do. He had to be.

"Mary, Mary," he sighed. "I used one of her stockings from the laundry basket. Her face was a picture. She looked up at me as if I was Jesus on the cross and she the penitent sinner. She was crying of course. It frustrated me. It was so ....," he paused for few seconds trying to conjure the right word, "pathetic. I said I wouldn't hurt her. But hey I lied. She begged for mercy, Mary. The hysterical crying was a dreadful noise. She needed to be put out of her misery, like an injured pet. So I picked up the stocking leant down as if to hug her and voila. It was just so easy. I pulled with all my might. What is the saying?" He looked around him trying to find the right words. "'It's as easy as 1, 2, 3.' She fell like a rag doll on the floor. I kicked the body a couple of times to be sure she was dead. Silence at last."

I tried to get up to leave the room but my legs felt like jelly I nearly reached the door when he grabbed my wrist. "You're hurting me, Michael. Let me go". His handcuffed hands then lifted to caress my face. I winced and tried to pull away from him. There was no struggle.

"Oh come, come. Please let me tell you the rest. I love a good story don't you?" I had no choice but to nod in agreement. I sat back down timidly.

"My father returned to the house to see a weeping boy lying across his dead mother. I left her naked. She didn't deserve dignity, the dirty bitch. My performance, Mary, was perfect. The sympathy people felt for me was so enjoyable. My father then started to drink and began to beat the shit out of me but was sent to prison not long after. I didn't think I'd be spending my school days in this cesspit. But think how excited I was to have that man right under my nose. I couldn't leave here without giving him my graduation gift could I?

"Oh and you, Mary," he said with glee, "you played your part so well. You were just perfect. So good in fact you deserve some applause." He clapped his hands slowly. "These make it so much more difficult to applaud," lifting his handcuffed hands.

I felt the tears in my eyes and a sickening feeling in my stomach. He moved round the desk and tried to wipe the tears from my face. I could feel the wet and texture of his bloody hands on me. I took a deep breath.

"What part? Why me?" I trembled.

"Oh so many questions, so little time before they," indicating the police outside the door, "come to take me away. I overhead you talking to Chad about your autistic brother. I knew I'd found you. I even felt a little sorry that I needed to use you. You exhibited compassion and caring for your brother that I felt you would do the same for a lonely, innocent child."

He removed his hands from my face, still leaning close to me, "You didn't disappoint Mary."

"What about the scars on your body?" I pointed to his chest.

"Such a small price to pay," he sighed. "All part of the master plan. You know I even started to believe my own insanity," he chuckle to himself.

"You cannot expect to get away with this."

"Well again, I'm counting on you for that." Again he gave a few seconds pause before he spoke again, "I'm sure that you won't disappoint."

"Did you start the fire, Michael?"

"You should be ashamed of yourself. Me! Start the fire. Now what do you think?"

"I don't know."

"No, Mary. That's not my style."

He pulled his chair to within inches of me, and took a hold of both my hands. He leaned in; his lips touching my hair. "You have the softest and sweetest smelling hair," he said as he sniffed the air.

"Dear Mary, when you told them of my disturbing behaviour and your great affection for me, they felt such compassion and sympathy for me. A stint in hospital is far better than being in jail. As you know, Mary, murders committed by children never see the splendour of a courtroom. As you know I was 11 years old and too young to be accountable. And the assault on the Head, I have a strong suspicion that these charges will be dropped."

I was still a little confused over the Headmaster's involvement; especially for the financial care of him. Why would he bring him to his school?

"Does he know that you saw you with your mother?"

"I believe so. He keeps me here locked up in fear that I will divulge his dirty secret. He was married to my mother's best friend. I haven't been expelled yet and as the saying goes 'keep your friends close but enemies closer.'"

"Why did you wait so long to take your revenge?"

"What's the fun in that? Keep him guessing; keep him afraid of me. Why did he not let me leave the grounds? It wasn't for my benefit."

"Where did you go when you disappeared?"

"I thought you might ask this. Well, I left the school before lights out and met a friend of mine in the local village. I stayed with her for a few days, partaking in a little extra-curricular activity, if you know what I mean. When I felt I had been away for a reasonable amount of time, I went back to the moor. I got thoroughly dirty and wet and then wandered aimlessly in the village like some lunatic until I was spotted by a do-good member of the public."

"Who is she?"

"No-one. Just someone I use from time to time."

I didn't wish to listen to any more. He began to stroke the side of my face again, wiping a tear from my face with the back of his hand. I visibly shuddered under his contact. I was shaking now and I felt incredible fear. He stared into my eyes it unnerved me. I had given every part of me to this boy. I had lost a fiancée, jeopardised my job, sent a good friend away and all the time I was being manipulated by this boy. I felt incredible shame that I had become entangled in his game.

"You have done so well, Mary. I just need you one more time."

He took both my hands into his and began to kiss the individual fingers. My tears were falling readily now.

"Just one more." I shook my head. "Oh I think you can, just for me. You love me, Mary. What would any mother do for their child? What will it be, Mary? Silent partners in crime or will you hand over the poor disturbed child to the police?"

I stood up, determined now to leave. He was asking me to be silent. Our secret: his mother's murder and now the death of the Headmaster.

"I trust you to do the right thing. You may go." He was so calm, his voice caressing his every word. He already knew my response.

I made my way to the door with as much dignity as I could muster but I feared my body would give me away. Tears now were streaming down my face, I knocked on the door. "Officer, we're finished now."

"Oh, Mary," I looked back at him, a sickening grin crossed his face, "I did enjoy the bath!"

I turned away, my body now shaking.

"Everything okay, Miss?" asked the constable outside the door.

I bit my bottom lip trying to stop the tears. All I managed a pitiful nod.

Dr Collins had returned to take Michael to the hospital. "We'll take care of him. We need to go now young man." He placed a gentle hand on Michael's shoulder. Michael slowly rose from his seat, and followed him out, his face sad and eyes staring. He walked past closely, deliberately rubbing his body against me. Where previously I felt warmth and comfort I now could only shudder at the closeness that he had manipulated. He paused at the front door. I could see the ambulance waiting for him. He turned to face me as he paused at the door. A huge smile crossed his face. He then lifted his hands to his to his face and with one last stare placed one finger to his lips.

And then he was gone.